CAUTION Men in Trees

CAUTION
Men in Trees

STORIES BY DARRELL SPENCER

The University of Georgia Press

Athens and London

Paperback edition published in 2010 by
The University of Georgia Press
Athens, Georgia 30602
www.ugapress.org
© 2000 by Darrell Spencer

Designed by Erin Kirk New
Set in 10 on 14 Berkeley Oldstyle Medium by G&S Typesetters

Printed digitally in the United States of America

The Library of Congress has cataloged the hardcover edition of this book as follows:
Library of Congress Cataloging-in-Publication Data
Spencer, Darrell, 1947–
    Caution, men in trees : stories / by Darrell Spencer.
        193 p. ; 21 cm.
    "Winner of the Flannery O'Connor award for short fiction"—P. preceding t.p.
    Contents: Park host—Blood work—There's too much news—The 12-inch
dog—Caution: men in trees—Late–night TV—Please to forgive sloppiness—It's a lot
scarier if you take Jesus out—Pronto bucks.
    ISBN 0-8203-2182-6 (alk. paper)
    1. West (U.S.)—Social life and customs—Fiction. I. Title.
PS3569.P446C38   2000
813'.54—dc21   99-35587
                            CIP

Paperback ISBN-13: 978-0-8203-3706-7
        ISBN-10: 0-8203-3706-4

British Library Cataloging-in-Publication Data available

Again, this one is for Kate, always;

and for Clark Hafen

CONTENTS

CAUTION Men in Trees

the very least, who's to blame. It's clear Krogh thinks Ygor and Dr. Frankenstein are in cahoots. Basil Rathbone plays the son. His pencil-line mustache is jittery. He snarls, "Is it the legendary monster of my father's time, or am I supposed to have whipped one up as a housewife whips up an omelet? I've been here a month, you know."

The Inspector confronts Frankenstein, irks him. All the time Basil's pitching darts at a dartboard, throwing bull's-eyes and retrieving them. "There's a monster afoot," Inspector Krogh says. "And you know it."

Basil flings darts, baits the Inspector toss after toss, needles the hell out of him, until the Inspector says, "You forget, I have my hat on."

The hat's a matter of form. Signifies official business.

"Meaning what," Basil says, "that I'm under arrest?"

The Inspector clicks his heels together and resets his wooden arm. Basil *is* under arrest.

So, on his way out of their camper this afternoon, Red says to Rose, "You forget. I have my hat on," and she, huddled close to the 13-inch Sony, which is jacked up loud, *Talk Back Live* on, says, "Then take it off." She's supposed to feed him Frankenstein's line.

Or ad-lib something equally droll.

Repartee.

Quid pro quo.

Quip for quip. Dart, as the movie would have it, for dart. Zinger for zinger.

One time she said, "What, you've got a monster up your butt?" She can be salty. She's said, "Hat, smat." And once, "Go tell it to the villagers."

Only a gooseneck lamp is on in the camper when Red says, "You forget, I have my hat on," and Rose says, "Then take it off."

The lamp's at Rose's side, on a tilt-top table, bent so it could be flesh-eating plant life sizing up her face.

These days, Rose keeps every rectangle of curtain shut. *Talk Back Live*, taking a break from the O. J. Simpson trial, is about the South Carolina woman who drowned her boys and then told the world a black man kidnapped them. Just babies, they were. Michael, three. Alex, a little over a year. The studio audience is forgiving her, saying what she did was not her doing, arguing it was not really the woman who strapped her boys in and let the car roll into the lake. It was the devil incarnate. They're claiming you have to distinguish act from person. Some lamebrain dressed head-to-toe in denim, a 9-inch daisy embroidered smack-dead-center on her chest, another daisy sewn to the crown of her floppy hat, this fool is saying, "Jesus can forgive. If Jesus can forgive her, where would I be with Jesus if I didn't forgive?"

As if she is Christ's personal friend.

Red hesitates on his way out the camper's door long enough to say, "Who died and made her our redeemer?"

Not a peep from Rose. She's been mopey and has wasted no words for weeks. Red and Rose, their talk's turned basic. You up. I'm up. Good. Do this. Do that. Curt and fundamental, that's Red and Rose Cogsby. Red misses their pillow talk, their comparing of notes. He's a man who relishes the bones they pick. Daily, Red fills the Prowler with the noise of his being, trusting against logic she'll take notice, and she's steadfastly aloof, sometimes icy. End result is Red feels like a beggar, like a clod wagging the dog's tail, hoping for a grin.

On the TV, a man gets to his feet and the woman who runs this show skips over and puts a mike in his face. He says, "God just borrowed to her the children. They back now with God."

Square his IQ and the man'd still be in trouble.

Red says to Rose, "Someone ought to check to see how much

of that guy's brain is actually missing in action." He resets his cap, tugging at its bill, fitting it solidly to his head. Is about to repeat his line, to say, "You forget, I have my hat on," when the savvy part of his brain, that seat of common sense and wisdom that got him through wind shear and dust storm back when he was flying the mail, warns him now is not the time.

Rose, glued to the TV, waves Red out of the camper, tells him she draped the kitchen throw rug over the picnic table to dry and if he brings it in now or later he's to shake it in case there are earwigs. "Look it up and down, front and back. Flap it good," she says. "And take out the birds." Used to be, before she took the blues to her heart, Rose'd have the budgies out by 7 A.M. Now they're still in their cage in a dark corner of the camper. One, Kathie Lee, is sour-apple green, and the other one, Regis, is sky-blue.

Rose and Red, they're here in Canyon Glen Park east of Provo, Utah. He's the park host, has been every summer for twenty-three years, and this afternoon he does have official business, it being July 6th, the day after the 5th, which was the day everyone celebrated the 4th because it fell on a Sunday and Utah shuts down for the Sabbath. Yesterday was, as Red's grandkids put things, the holiday from hell. Someone reported a man carrying a gun, and five sheriffs in five 4-Runners showed up, ex-football types carrying shotguns, nervous sullen men who concentrated on the ground and their own feet. One had a Remington sniper rifle. Turned out the man with a gun was a man with a camera. Must have been three hundred people in campgrounds fit for one-third that number. The Utah Boys Ranch delivered carloads full of juvenile delinquents. One ran away and wasn't located until dark. Another one lost his temper and, given his limited and crude perspective on the world, didn't know what the civilized thing to do was, so he tore his clothes off and sat naked on a picnic table. Red kept chasing after kids and their firecrackers, but caught no one.

So, on his way out, Red collects the budgies, and, hiking their cage onto a shoulder, uses his foot to nudge the Prowler's door open, which is so narrow and otherwise dinky and flimsy it always reminds him of the door to the pisser on an airplane. He juggles the budgies' cage, gets leverage and a firmer grip, eases it through the door, stands on the footstool they use as a step, and says to Rose, "If you look in the local section of last night's paper you'll find an article that tells you how to keep earwigs out of your garden."

"A duck is how," she says.

Damn, but she knows stuff. Red's taken again by the miscellany Rose has up her sleeve. "That sounds good to me," he says. "I didn't read it," and he leans in for a final look, anticipation in his left eye and optimism in his right. Shows no fear of her wretched melancholy. Hope is the horse he rides.

And she speaks to him.

"Hate those things," Rose says. She means the earwigs.

"They are one of God's ugliest creatures," Red says. He shifts the budgies' cage around and resets his legs for balance.

She says, "They're like something big made small, so out of spite they end up ugly and underfoot, like a dinosaur brought to its knees, made to say uncle." She puts her hand to her mouth as if she's checking it for puffiness.

"You got that right," he says.

Smart as an encyclopedia, Rose is, and she used to rise early and whistle tunes. Now she's a killjoy. The overriding problem seems to be the dark cloud called the O. J. Simpson trial. She's up to her elbows in it. Is angry. Is getting peeved about what she sees as justice going down the tubes. All day she watches the trial, crept into a corner or is disgusted. Red can hear the TV. "Rose speak to you?" he says to Regis. The bird scrambles up a ladder, gets beak to nose with him. Red says, "Do you know what the problem is?"

Kathie Lee says, "What's up?"

"Your guess," Red says, "is as good as mine." He sprays the misty water above the cage, and it falls like the gentlest of rains. Kathie Lee pulls a feather loose, says, "Good show."

Inside, Red locates his Colt and wrangles himself into a shoulder holster. He looks like a gangster. Rose has asked him not to wear the getup in the park. Someone always calls the cops. The TV's so loud Red doesn't say a word to her. He cuts up another apple and takes it to the budgies, then ties a rope around a hitch on a pump and drags the outfit down to the river, where he attaches fifty feet of leaky fire hose. The pump generates enough pressure that he can spray down the park's central pavilion. He'll clean it twice today. A family named Johannson reserved it from noon to six. Then a Scout troop's scheduled it from seven to ten. Done, Red waters a couple of dry spots in the grass, then hauls the pump to the other side of the river, couples another twenty-five feet of hose to the hose he's already laid out, and angles the nozzle so it will flood the clearing north of his and Rose's campsite. He's got three hours before the water reaches the rest rooms near the Prowler.

Some jerk let domestic rabbits loose in the park, and one sits on a knoll watching Red. It's the brown of milk chocolates. Rose feeds them. Or she did. Lately she's left her chores to Red. She's also abandoned the rest rooms. It's Red who sprinkles Comet and scrubs the sinks and toilets. For the rabbits, he buys pellets at the Petsmart in town. Rose counted five, two lop-ears and three she didn't recognize. They don't have a chance in the park. Can't fend for themselves. They're pets, for God's sake, Rose says.

Up the river, Red stops for another smoke. Nine left in his pack. Rate he's going this afternoon he'll be borrowing on tomorrow's allotment before he climbs into bed. He stands on a concrete bridge that crosses a steep bend in the river. There's serious white water here. The canyon's asphalt trail passes behind him. It begins fifteen miles away at Utah Lake, curves alongside the river through two cities to this point, then continues for another four miles, weaving through Nunn's Park, before it reaches Bridal Veil Falls. There's also a grid of trails in the glen below Red. He can see the pavilion to his right. To his left is a larger clearing where two summers ago he built a backstop for baseball. The diamond amounts to bare spots kids have worn in the grass, dirt marking the base pads. There's a half-assed game going on, two girls at bat, and three more in the outfield. Softball.

Bobcat Hair and the woman cross the clearing, their dog, not on a leash, sniffing at the girls. The pitcher twists her cap around backward and frowns at the dog. Red stubs out his cigarette, adds it to his tin. Checks his pack. He miscounted. Only seven left. He follows the trail until it meets a gravel road that borders the clearing. He drops through a grove of cottonwoods and can see Bobcat Hair, the woman, and their dog. She's carrying her sandals. Bobcat Hair is wearing black harness boots, and he's taken his shirt off. The number nine is tattooed on both his arms near his wrists. The dog's only a puppy. Red retrieves a plastic bag from where it's stuck itself to a bench leg and tosses it in the trash, lights a Camel and walks toward them.

The woman tries to catch hold of Bobcat Hair's arm. Most likely she wants him to take stock of the fact that this man smoking the Camel is armed, but Bobcat Hair, he pulls away, says to Red, "What's your problem?"

Red sucks hard on his cigarette. The Colt rests against his ribs, comfortable, offering a glimpse of itself.

He says, "Has Rose been out?" The birds tilt their heads, puzzled. He checks the throw rug for earwigs, then tucks it under his arm. Regis flies to the ladder and, upside down, climbs its rungs. Red sprays mist above the cage, and Kathie Lee says, "We wish you a Merry Christmas. We wish you a Merry Christmas."

Red knocks sharply on the Prowler's door before he steps inside. It's one of Rose's most recent requests. Doesn't Red know why they invented doors? she wants to know. He doesn't have to wait for *come in*. Just knock. That's all she's asking for. Rose is yelling at the TV. "DNA can't fly," she says. She calls someone a horse's ass. O. J.'s back on.

"Did you eat yet?" Red says.

There's an empty cereal bowl sitting in the light of the gooseneck on the tilt-top table. Looks like she's had Wheaties. The bowl ought to be soaking.

He says, "Rug's fine. No earwigs," and he flattens it to the floor in the kitchen area.

"Justice takes a holiday," Rose says, and she jabs the remote at the Sony, kills the sound. "Earl Tall sent you a note," she says. She points at the kitchen counter. "Some kid brought it to the door, one of those lunatics on skates. Starts banging on the door so the birds are screaming, and I'm not going to bother, but then he's hollering. Tall must've told him our name. He's saying, 'Mr. Cogsby. Mr. Cogsby.' So I went so he'd shut up." She punches up the sound, catches Larry King saying, "Hold that thought. We'll be right back."

The note's folded in half. Earl Tall is asking Red to come see him at his campsite. *It's important*, Earl writes. Red says to Rose, "I think I'll go for chicken. You want to come?" He's thinking he'll bring some to Earl, and he's wondering if important means urgent or worth his while.

Rose waves Red off, says, "Already eaten."

Piss-poor idea of eating, he thinks.

It'll be dark if he drives into town, runs errands, and buys the chicken, so he puts together a peanut-butter-and-jelly sandwich and starts for the door.

"Your gun," Rose says.

Red says, "I got some questions for Earl. About the trigger and loading it."

"In the abstract," she says. "Ask him in the abstract. You don't need to do show-and-tell. You scare people, and I don't want cops disrupting my evening. Draw pictures for him."

Red gulps his sandwich. In their bedroom, he gets free of the holster and sneaks the pistol into his back pocket. His windbreaker covers it. Earl Tall and Red, they've known each other something over ten years. They met here in the canyon, only to learn they both live in Bountiful, Utah. Every summer Earl reserves a space in Nunn's the first two weeks of July. He camps alone, gets away from the wife, Eva, and their boys, who've got their own families but who built houses only half a block away from Eva and Earl. Red and Earl have guns in common. Earl worked as a pistol smith when he was younger. Back in the city, the two of them volunteer as Santa Clauses every year—even, for the hell of it, went to Tom Valent's famous Santa Claus school, drove themselves to Midland, Michigan, where they learned the basics, which are Never Flirt, Never Drink, Never Smoke. The biggest mistake you can make is too much *yo* and not enough *ho*. Still, theirs is one of those nonpersonal, now-and-then friendships. Except for the Santa Clausing, they don't see each other in Bountiful. No get-togethers with the wives. It's like they keep the good footing they offer each other separate from family.

The evening's hot, so once Red hits the trail to Nunn's he folds up the windbreaker and carries it. It's a twenty-minute walk. He hugs the shade to the south side of the trail. There are a few joggers, but mostly couples strolling. He sees one of the pet rabbits down by the river. It's brown and white, spotted the way pintos are and lop-eared. It looks worried.

A small hill lowers the trail into Nunn's. The river borders the park on its north side, and an asphalt road circles through it. There are twenty-two campsites. Red plans to check permits before he leaves. Most of the families are picnicking and will be gone before ten, but there are four places booked for the night. He can see some pup tents. Near one, a husky is tethered to a tree, and in the clearing next to it a young couple are eating dinner, sitting on blankets. They're both wearing baseball caps. Red's about to cross to the other side of the trail when he hears "Passing" and a bike rider whips by his shoulder. They come out of nowhere. You look behind you. Nothing there. All's clear. You're safe. Then you take a step toward the other side, and a bike's on top of you.

Earl's in site twelve, the first one off the trail at this end of the park. It's back in the trees. He drives an old VW van he's cut down and welded a camper shell to. You can stand full height inside. He's added bunk beds, and there's a refrigerator and a stove. His mountain bike bolts on above the front bumper.

Red finds Earl down by the river where he's shaking leaves from a tarp. Earl's wearing bushwhacker shorts and no shirt. He's barefoot, his boots and socks on the site's redwood table. He's kept the white beard he grew last Christmas.

"Too much *yo*, not enough *ho*," Red says before Earl sees him.

Earl whacks the tarp like he hates it, then spreads it across one end of the table and grabs Red's hand. He tugs Red in and claps his back. He says, "Don't smoke."

Red says, "Don't drink."

"Don't flirt."

"No neck jewelry."

Earl steps aside. "You came," he says.

Red says, "Was there a question that Red Cogsby would?"

"Only in my head," Earl says.

Red unwedges the pistol from his back pocket and says, "Can you take a look at this?" It's a Gold Cup, Series 70. Red tells Earl he plans to replace the sear and hammer, maybe the trigger. He heard that you can, but he's not sure he trusts the source of that information, an ex-cop.

Earl says, "Let's go take a load off. Coffee's on." He checks his tarp, straightens one end. He takes the Colt from Red, saying, "You do the sear and hammer and you'll want to replace the slide, too." At the front of the VW, Earl collects a dead rattlesnake he's hooked over his mountain bike's handlebars. He dangles it between them. Earl chopped its head off. It's probably four feet long and as thick as his forearm. "That's my third one already," he says.

"They're bad as insects this year," Red says.

Earl says, "I wouldn't mind if they bit a few of these idiots on bicycles, would you?" He tosses the snake into some cotton-woods.

"Not on your life."

Inside, Red and Earl sit in canvas tent chairs and talk guns. Earl's coffee's thick as tar. He spikes it, though, Johnnie Walker scotch whiskey. Earl shows Red the Colt revolver he bought in North Carolina. It's one of the famous Peacemakers. He digs in a drawer, comes up with cartridges, and loads the revolver. Like he's holding a tray, he displays it for Red, says, "You want it?"

Red's comfortable around guns, only he doesn't like this one being loaded. Doesn't know why Earl did that, why he'd bother. His Colt, unloaded, sits in his lap on his windbreaker. Red says, "How much are you asking?"

"I'm not asking, except for the biggest favor you've ever done a man," Earl says.

"What's that?"

Earl gestures for Red to heft the gun, to get a feel for its weight and balance. Red takes it, and Earl says, "Alzheimer's runs in families." Earl sits back, says, "You can have your genotype done, and you'll know the sorry or good news. Some people know that's possible. That you can find out, if you want. Did you?"

Red offers him the revolver. He won't take it, so Red sets it on the floor between his feet. Red says, "Rose'd know."

"Of course she would."

"She could tell you the details."

"I got two brothers, both dead from it," Earl says. "My sister needs twenty-four-hour-a-day care. She doesn't remember how to button her own clothes. She believes her teeth are tombstones. Wicked people are buried in her mouth."

"All this is terrible news," Red says.

"The terrible news is I have it," Earl says.

Red looks at his feet, one foot on each side of the revolver. He looks at Earl's bare feet.

"Twice now I've started for one place and ended up states and days away from where I was going," Earl says. "It's happened months apart, but it's happened."

"You're exaggerating."

"Only a little."

"Could be our age, Earl," Red says. "What you're describing sounds like something I do every day."

"You've found yourself a thousand miles from where you meant to be?"

"Not quite."

"Forgetting to take out the garbage isn't the same."

"Don't they say, 'If you think you've got it, you don't?'"

"The day I came here, I was about settled in, when my son drives up," Earl says. "I'm thinking, what's he doing here? He's never come down before. Not once, in—what?—ten years. He tells me—he says, 'Dad, I was visiting a buddy in Provo and stopped to say hello.' I say right to his face, 'Bullshit,' and he acts like I slugged him. I say, 'Your mother sent you because all of you think I might have driven to Nebraska.'"

Earl gets out of his chair. He's talking, and he starts knocking books and tools from the shelves. He turns over a chair. He doesn't look angry, and he doesn't sound angry. It's like he's practiced what he's doing. Like he's in a play. He's pictured in his head how he'll do it. He says, "I told my boy that if he was going to look after his father he'd need to know how to change diapers because that's what it's going to come to." Earl opens a drawer in the one chest he has and dumps out cards, screws, pens, paper. He yanks clothes from two other drawers. He's ransacking his place. "I read in a magazine," he says, "where one man forgot how to use his utensils. His knife, his fork and spoon, could have been rocks. When he did get food in, it sat in his mouth. He'd forgotten how to chew."

Earl kicks a throw rug to the side of his chair, and Red scoots back. The revolver's there on the floor. "That's a true story," Earl says. "I can show you the magazine." He stands in front of Red and says, "A month ago I woke up, peed okay, but looked in the bathroom mirror and had no idea how to shave. I knew I needed to shave, understood the obligation I had, but I couldn't have done it if you'd have given me the Chinese torture." He squats and picks up the revolver, checks the chamber, and offers it to Red, says, "Which is what I want you to do, my friend."

Red won't take the gun.

"But right here," Earl says, and he touches his chest where his heart is. "Three bullets."

His sadness cuts up Red.

Red says, "I won't do that no matter what you say you have, even if you prove it."

"It's a robbery," Earl says and he gestures toward the mess he's made. "I worked it out," Earl says. "Come back tonight and take whatever you want. I'll help you." He finds a pillowcase and opens it. "We'll fill this with stuff," he says. "I own a coin collection I brought along. Take all the guns." He drops the pillowcase, says, "Who would ever know?"

Red gets up and stuffs his Colt into his back pocket. He climbs into his windbreaker.

Earl pokes the revolver at Red. Earl's got his white beard and his white chest hair. He's tan. "I need you to do this," Earl says. "The time's coming when I won't exist anymore. Who am I if I don't recognize myself? Can you understand that?"

"We're just who we are," Red says.

"No," Earl says. He turns the handle of the revolver toward Red and says, "Take it."

Red does. This is the Colt that won the West. Its balance is a thing you can't match.

"It's a wonderful shooting iron," Earl says. "All you have to do is come back after dark. There's no moon tonight. I checked. You can see on the calendar. No one will see you."

Red says, "I couldn't for any reason."

"The man forgot how to chew," Earl says. He chomps his teeth together. "I read about it in that magazine. He thought his grandson was an owl. He talked to bushes."

Red backs out the door like he's the one who's about to be shot, and he places the revolver on the camper steps. Earl's crying.

Last thing Red says to him is "Sorry." Earl doesn't need Red's advice, which is, Let the bad news settle. He doesn't want Red to tell him how stupid he's acting, how sorry he'd be.

The sky above the mountains to the west is white. It'll be dark in half an hour. Red notices Bobcat Hair's wife outside a tent they've put up. They've started a fire, circled it with rocks. There's no camping here, not in this area. Hero the dog is roaming in the clearing. Red gets a piece of rope from his truck and brings it to the wife. "I think this will work on the dog," he says, and he hands the rope to her.

"That's nice of you," she says. "We're sort of between good times."

Red shows her how to tie a clove hitch. There's a tree close to the tent, and they hook the dog to it. "If he'll allow it," Red says, "you'd be better off keeping the dog inside with you."

"The dog?" she says.

Red says, "Your husband, if your husband will let you."

She says, "He won't."

Red says, "Have you got something to eat?"

"We do."

"Because we've got plenty," Red says.

"We're just fine. Thank you."

"If you need anything," Red says, "let me know," and he heads for the Prowler.

Two weeks later it's Rose who points out Earl's obituary in the *Tribune*. She mutes the television and reads out loud to Red. "Seventeen grandkids, if you can believe that," she says. "He's got family spread all over the place." Red wonders how he died, and she tells him the paper didn't say. He puts in a few phone calls. Accidental, he is told. While Earl was cleaning his guns.

My foot, Red thinks.

The day of the funeral the O. J. Simpson trial is in recess, and Red talks Rose into driving up to Bountiful with him. It rained seriously all night, then quit at sunrise. They'll be gone most of the day so they leave the budgies in the trailer. Red opens the curtains, notices furniture he hasn't seen for weeks. Everything's dusty. In the sunlight, Kathie Lee says, "Life in the fast lane." Regis pecks at the music box in his cage, and it begins *Love Me Tender*. Regis sings along, sounds a lot like Elvis himself. Kathie Lee butts in, adds, "Love me sweet."

Rose and Red take their new GM truck. The drive is two hours, and Rose, she studies the Wasatch Mountains like they contain the hallelujah of all creation, as if they stand for all that is trustworthy, are truly God's handiwork. Red mentions the budgies and their distress. She doesn't blink. He tries the weather as an icebreaker. "They say this is the leading edge of a rain train," he says. She gives him her coldest shoulder. He shuts up. Once bitten, twice shy.

Rose stares at the heavens washed clean by the rain, or she reads, a book on DNA. Red knits together the bits and pieces of his life up to this minute here in this truck on I-15 driving to the funeral of Earl Tall. Wonders what turns he took he shouldn't have. Wonders if he could have jumped up and down more. Rose taught the budgies that Robert Frost poem everyone learns in school, the one about the fork in the road, and how you regret you can't travel both of them and experience wherever it is they take you, the point being you have to make choices. It took her a year, and the birds, they've got it down pat.

What if Red'd shot Earl Tall?

What if he'd done his pal that favor?

He calculates the cost, adds pro to con, weighs debt against request. Plus or minus, Red can't decide. Even in the abstract.

Rose videotaped Kathie Lee and Regis reciting the Frost poem. They do it word for word. No mistakes. On film, they sway like '50s rock and roll singers.

The cemetery's soaked, water puddles on the grass, and the mortuary laid down plywood for the mourners to walk across. Earl Tall is buried with full military honors. Nine old duffers, potbellied, all wearing army-green shirts and army-brown trousers, aviator glasses, and bolo ties and standing like clothespins, present arms and fire three rounds, their rifles dropping lower with each shot. They stand in a street that enters the cemetery, and their spent cartridges ping when they hit the pavement. A little girl begins crying. One of the veterans steps forward and plays taps. Two others remove the American flag from the casket, fold it military fashion, and present it to Eva Tall.

Red catches up to her when she's leaving. Her sons, bulky men, stand at her side. Grandkids blast in and out, mud on their shoes, mud spotting their trousers. Eva wears a pillbox hat. It has a veil. "I served with Earl in Korea," Red says to her. It's a lie. As bald-faced as a lie can be. He's betting Earl didn't talk much to Eva about him. Eva tucks her handkerchief up her sleeve and gathers in the handshake Red offers, her grip soft as a daylily's would be.

"I'm sorry. We've met," she says. "You're from the canyon, but I don't know your name."

"I'm Red Cogsby," Red says. "I was an orderly in the war, like on that TV show, and your husband was the best surgeon they had. Under those conditions, no one could hold a candle to him."

"I appreciate your telling me that," she says.

BLOOD WORK

The Mormon lady next door tells J. J. Cribb she put his hamstring in their temple. It's a curious way to express what she sees as the voucher of her goodwill, but he understands what she means. J. J.'s not been in Salt Lake City for more than two days in the last five years, did grow up here, though, and his mother was Mormon from the word go, an affiliation she often and happily announced. For the last twenty-three years she was alive, she drove herself to the temple twice a week and did temple work. One of her duties was to pray for the sick of every stripe, the halt and lame of mind, body or spirit. J. J.'s hamstring *is* sore, could, in certain ways, be thought of as sick.

The Mormon temple is a scale model of the universe, boxed to the compass, its cornerstones laid clockwise in the ground. It stands as a point of order in the face of chaos. Only the most worthy Mormons get in, and there they perform sacred ordinances. Their church leaders ask that you and the local newspapers call members Latter-day Saints, not Mormons.

J. J.'s dad, Samuel Cribb Jr., tells J. J. you don't talk to the neighbor lady unless you've got a lawyer by your side. Hire one, if you have to. She and her family—her husband, three teenage girls and a boy—moved in soon after J. J., his first divorce one day under his belt, moved to Henderson, Nevada. Samuel Cribb's not addressed a civil word to any of the family, and he has no plans to. "Not even after the last dog's been hung," he says.

The neighbor lady's name's Flora. Husband's Leonard, a CPA who keeps accounts for the Mormons and restores vintage convertibles. Flora's russet hair falls like an A-frame from the top of her head, and she has those reptilian eyes. She wears no makeup. J. J. guesses she's sixty, but she could be fifty. There's a measure of dread like a night lamp in her face. Claim around the neighborhood is she's no fun, is full of mood.

Yesterday, she introduced herself to J. J. just as he finished his morning run. He'd turned the corner two blocks up from his dad's place and felt that hamstring nip and tweak he knew too well, that mid-stride out-of-the-blue kick to the backside of the thigh, not the rip that knocks you to your knees, but the lodging of a complaint. He down-geared into a trot-and-shuffle, the onland equivalent of a dog paddle. The street below dropped away steep enough to knock you cartwheeling if you misstepped. A running buddy has told J. J. he is too tightly wound, has recommended yoga, but only *after* a run, has argued for nightclub dancing and yelling in the shower. Has suggested screaming at traffic from overpasses.

J. J. didn't see Flora. He slowed from his trot-and-shuffle to a half-assed poke-along and then walked from the corner to the fence that separated his father's yard from hers, and she stepped from the shadows between the two houses. By then, he had hoisted his foot up so his heel rested on the low cinder block fence that ran from her backyard to the sidewalk, and J. J. was flexing his leg. Ivy covered most of the fence. She said, "My guess is it's your hamstring."

"I'm afraid so," J. J. said. He leaned toward his foot and felt the hamstring protest.

"Probably the downhills we've got here," Flora said.

J. J. flexed his leg, swung it into place so he was standing on both feet, and said, "Probably. It's happened before." He told her he'd never run hills well, up or down, but especially not down, couldn't let go no matter how eloquently he sweet-talked his brain into relaxing. J. J. brakes and fights against loosening and lengthening his stride, runs instead like he's jammed cue balls into his arches. He pictures in his head as incentive and hero that Keep on Truckin' guy, but doing so does no good. A downhill comes, and he sort of checks up, like a ratchet. He knows better. He's read the articles. He's lost months of running to his bad hamstring.

Flora was cutting to stalks the daylilies and rudbeckia that border her yard, readying them for winter. She set her scissors on the cinder block wall and said, "Worse thing you can do is to run hills too slow rather than too fast." She tugged off her cotton gloves and placed them next to the scissors. "My boy," she said, "runs cross-country for West High. *Sports* magazine ranked the team number one in the country." She used her hands to show J. J. the hills and gullies, the uncivilized trails, the swoop and drop, swag and pitch that come with running through fields. She said, "You watch the joggers who go by here, and they fight the downhill like they're in danger of it rising up and smacking them. Especially the men, for some reason. They jab at the road. On their face is that look you see on people who are putting a big toe in the swimming pool to see if they really want to go for a dip. You'd think the men are afraid they're going to fly off the planet. The women, for the most part, they glide past our place."

J. J. told her he'd been running at sea level. "Up here," he said, "I'm not sure I'm getting oxygen to my muscles like I should."

"That's likely. It happens."

J. J. explained that he was Samuel's son, was Samuel Cribb, Junior Junior. The family, to keep phone calls and messages straight, first called him Cribb, then Junior Junior, which of course quickly turned into J. J. Sometimes, for a joke, his dad was simply J.

Flora said she'd never actually talked to J. J.'s father, which at the time surprised J. J. because although there was no logic to forge any kind of connection or friendship the house Flora lived in had been Lester Hirsch's, J. J.'s father's lifelong friend and smoking buddy, two, as they described themselves, reprobate run-to-seed Mormons, born to the faith and a lifetime of agile sidestepping it. Jack Mormons, that's what the Latter-day Saints once called such members. Now they'd be referred to politely as inactives, except Hirsch died.

J. J. himself had walked away from it all when he was seventeen. He'd gotten up in the middle of a Mormon sacrament meeting, excused himself as he picked his way toward an aisle, and left through the front door. The speaker, a church leader in the area, was talking about Satan, saying, especially for the ears, hearts, and minds of the young people, that Satan talks softly. Try this small wrong, Satan whispers. Smoke this cigarette, Satan says. Then he's got you by the throat. Let's steal something, he says. Let's buy porn. Let's shoot up. Small wrongs lead to greater wrongs. J. J. studied the man, his gray suit and tie, his white shirt, his salt-and-pepper haircut and arrested, insignia hair, hair like a flagship, and recognized that if there was a Satan he was looking at the man, that if there was a Satan he was listening to his soft tongue. Satan would be the picture of civility. He'd dress and talk *bona fides*, whole truths and nothing but the truths. Butter wouldn't melt in his mouth.

The sidewalk squares are uprooted and neglected. They look jerry-built and seem confused about their basic function. His route zigzags him about a mile and a half toward the center of the city, first south down one of the short alphabet streets and then west across one of the avenues, so it's one block breakneck incline, say down M, then across a block, say Fourth Avenue, which is only somewhat downhill. Then south again down headlong L Street, J. J. knowing better but holding his stride in check, restrained and reined in, jabbing, as Flora said, at the pavement, and then he can relax and breeze across Third Avenue, followed next by the tight-assed downhill of K, then easy sailing along Second Avenue.

The houses throughout the neighborhoods are catch-as-catch-can. You name a type of architecture and you'll see it. They're jig-sawed together, maybe five feet apart from garage to the neighbor's kitchen window. Eventually, J. J. comes out on South Temple where the Governor's Mansion sits under repair. A Christmas-light fire gutted it two years ago. From here the city flattens gradually, and J. J. runs west toward downtown. Now he sticks to the sidewalks. They're still uneven and crazy with edges, but safer than the traffic, which is four-laned and hotheaded.

Today, a red light catches J. J. next to the Hotel Utah, and he jogs in place. He's kitty-corner to the Mormon temple. J. J. imagines his hamstring in there, women like his mother, like Ruby, ministering to it. Thick women whose carriage is both humble and proud. These are the meek who shall inherit the earth. They are sober and grim. Dignified. Serene. Even their hair is solid as a rock. Their eyes radiate love. Pure light encircles them. No one talks. They rub balm in. Ointments. Aloe. A woman with a nurse's touch applies a poultice. All of it—it's soothing. The toxins flee. The women who look like Ruby kneel and pray. Unction, Piety, Grace, Hope, these are their names.

Against the traffic, antsy, J. J. skips, sidesteps, quibbles his way across Main Street and runs hard along the wide sidewalk that borders Temple Square. You could drag race at least two cars on it. Temple Square covers a two-acre block. People who come to Salt Lake praise the city's lack of trash and wonder if Mormons are citizens of the United States. It's a fair question, if you think about it. The granite wall around their temple must be twenty feet high. Inside there is the temple itself, and there is the Tabernacle, where the Mormon Tabernacle Choir sings. There is a visitors center where you can ask your questions. Guides will give you pamphlets and Books of Mormon. You can see films about the church. If you leave your name, they'll send missionaries to teach you the gospel. Or you can refer them to friends. You speak French? They'll send French-speaking missionaries. Russian? Dutch? Navajo? No problem. They've got people who speak the language.

Every day, J. J. circles Temple Square and heads back to his father's. This way he puts in four tough miles, up and down hills. J. J. did his homework when he was a kid, figured, in a teenager's way, that if you were going to build a life on religious belief you ought to know its history. No riding on anyone's coattails for J. J. He took his Mormonism seriously until the day he, as Ruby put it, bowed out. So he read and studied. He knows, for one thing, the New York Times once described the temple as frowning. The Times said it was barbaric in its refusal to conform to any known school of architecture. It looks Gothic, but isn't. Three towers stand at both the east and the west entrances, each central tower higher than the other two. The temple's built of granite quarried from Little Cottonwood Canyon. The angel Moroni, gold-leafed and fourteen feet high, stands on its capstone blowing his trumpet to announce that God's word has been restored to the earth. One story goes that when the angel was lowered into place on top of the 210-foot central tower on the east side, the church's president, Wilford Woodruff, turned to the man who'd sculpted the statue and said, "Now, Mr. Dallin, do you believe in angels?" Cyrus Dallin replied, "Yes, my mother is an angel."

The temple's facade is covered with icons. There are sunstones and moonstones. There are fifty earth stones that show the seven-days-of-the-week rotation of the earth. Fifty moonstones work out the cycle of the lunar month. There are star stones and Saturn stones, and there is the all-seeing eye of God. There is God's declaration I AM ALPHA AND OMEGA, and a dedicatory inscription begins HOLINESS TO THE LORD.

J. J. heads toward the state capitol building when he gets back to State Street. It's a gut-check climb. His knees hurt. He weaves through traffic, crosses to the sidewalk on the other side of the street. Behind him, somewhere on a spire of the temple, is Ursa Major, the Big Dipper, carved into the granite. According to Truman Angell, the temple's architect, it has a moral, which is that the lost may find themselves by the Priesthood of God. J. J. knows we stand before the temple the way we stand before the heavens. We get our bearings from it. His running in the shadow of the temple is a test of his stride, foot strike, and knee bend, the set of his elbow and the rocking-chair swing of his arm . Ruby used to tell him everything on earth is a matter of comportment. She believed in decorum, in good manners, in posture. How you sit in a chair is how you'd sit in the throne of God were you given the chance. How you eat is how you would eat in the presence of Deity. How you shovel. How you sweep. How you walk. Etiquette was more than a word.

Head down, J. J. chugs up North State. It's a clean-air day. He phoned to make sure. His lungs are safe. This trash-free city is under threat to lose federal funding if it doesn't clean up its pollution. Near the top, J. J. feels his hamstring knot itself, and he stops to stretch, one foot up on the curb, one foot in the gutter. He does both legs. He takes the easy downhill to his left, then turns north again past the Pioneer Memorial Museum. The state capitol building's on his right. The climb is extreme, and he can't do anything but lean forward and focus on the road. His chest, it seems, is almost touching the pavement. He turns east and is walking by the time he rests at the top of 500 North.

Across Capitol Boulevard is the entrance to City Creek Canyon. Signs say DO NOT ENTER, WRONG WAY. They're for cars, and the way they're posted they seem angry. Everyone runs here, in both directions. Used to be this was called Gravity Hill, was a place Samuel introduced J. J. to. This is where dads brought their kids to wow them. Couples stopped here to grab at each other. It was open to traffic both ways back then. You'd park at the entrance at what looks like it's the top, and your dad'd point out how steep it seemed to be, how it appeared like you were headed directly downhill. "Take a look," your dad would say, and the kids'd peer out the windshield or hang from a side window. Dad puts the car in neutral, says, "Keep your eyes peeled and a free hand on your heart," and gloats when his big Oldsmobile starts to roll the wrong way, when it starts to roll backward in the direction of what must be uphill. The dad says, "That's one for the books." He says, "That's something to write home about."

J. J. cruises through the canyon. Here and there, at bends in the road, he can see downtown. Salt Lake's building itself a skyline. At the bottom, where the skinny road horseshoes over City Creek and a concrete dam so that now you're climbing Lake Bonneville Boulevard back up into the avenues, J. J. hesitates, thinking that somewhere along here is a road that follows the river, that winds through Memory Grove, thinking if he can locate it he'll take it through the park so, looping back, he comes out near North State and the temple, adding a mile to his run. He's not paying attention when a car flies around the corner and skids toward him. He hops off the asphalt, turns his ankle, and is flung down the grade fifteen, twenty feet on his butt. Kids in the car yell, but J. J. hears only what sounds like a shot goose. He's almost in the creek. He rolls so he can sit, and his ankle throbs. He picks gravel from his hand. He takes off his shoe, scoots down the bank, and eases the injured ankle into the cold water. He slips his hand into the river. The water's numbing. Five minutes, then he takes off his T-shirt and dries the foot, pulls sock and shoe on, and tightens the lace so it will slow the circulation. He gets into his T-shirt. It's pleasantly damp. J. J. limps to the road, then walks slowly up Bonneville, tries trotting—it's okay—so he begins to run. The ankle's fine, but his hand burns, like he's broken a blood vessel.

Rather than a hunt-and-peck jog down the alphabet streets and across the avenues so that he works his way like a crossword puzzle from C Street to M Street, from 11th Avenue to 6th Avenue, J. J. stays with 11th until he comes to M, then he lopes down it. He waves at a bearded guy on his porch, expects—why, he doesn't know—to get the finger in return, but the guy just stares. There's ice and indifference here, but also an intelligence that could pocket you and the nine ball in an unheard of combination. The man's beard is the color of bitter-sweet chocolate. His eyes measure you for a coffin. He'd eat your young for breakfast. He is smoking a cigar, and there is a 35-mm camera on the porch railing. He's a man who, seated front row center or behind a pillar in the balcony, could upset the Peking Acrobats and their tower of chairs. This man knows how far we as people are truly open to deceit and illusion.

J. J. slows between Third Street and Fourth Street and is walking by the time he reaches the corner. Flora, planting bulbs in her front yard, sits back and says, "Your knee?"

J. J. glances down. His knee's been bleeding. The blood is dark, looks like a failed *S*. He says, "I fell."

"That will happen," she says.

The *Tribune*'s lying at the bottom of his dad's porch steps. J. J. snags the newspaper and wonders if Flora will put his knee in the temple.

J. J.'s hand is swollen, but no longer hurts. Looks as if he's shoved a walnut under the skin where his pinkie meets his knuckle. He stands at the kitchen sink, runs cold water on the swelling, and watches Samuel dig around the base of a maple that's started life too close to the back fence. He's digging with a long-bladed tool, one you'd use for flowers, and is working so slowly he could be forty years at this job. Birds hopscotch on his feeders. They nip into tubes of sunflower seeds. J. J. pours a glass of orange juice and takes it outside. Samuel's portable oxygen tank is lying in the grass at his side, but he's not using it. He's hooked the cannula around his neck so the tubing trails down his back.

J. J. comes up behind his dad and says, "Let me give you a break."

Samuel leans on his hands. His face is flushed. He's sweaty.

"One hundred percent pure Florida orange juice," J. J. says and offers his dad the glass.

Samuel takes it.

The roots of the maple run under the fence. Samuel's already dug another hole for replanting it. He and J. J. marked a spot where there were no power or phone lines running overhead, and it won't crowd the spruce Samuel planted in the spring.

J. J. says, "Rest a minute," and he reaches for the spade.

Samuel waves him away, saying, "I need to get as much root as possible." He hands J. J. the empty glass and starts chopping at the hole. "See those fingers trailing off under the fence, like thread," he says. "We need them. We don't want to cut any off."

"Will it live?" J. J. says.

Samuel says, "There's no way I know of to tell." He pulls at the base of the tree. It's loose. J. J. bends over, gets a grip about a third of the way up the young trunk—can, for the first time, feel serious pain in his hand—and pulls while his father chops at the dirt. The roots give, then release.

"Got it," J. J. says.

They replant the tree, Samuel tamping, J. J. shoveling. The hole three-quarters full, Samuel dumps in fertilizer. He fills it with water that quickly seeps in. J. J. spades more dirt into the hole, and Samuel spreads it evenly. No way is the tree going to make it. They might as well be planting a fence post. J. J. and Samuel stand, dust themselves off, and Samuel unfolds a piece of paper he's pulled from his back pocket. He's removed the cannula and set it and his oxygen on the back steps. He begins to read. "Job 14," he says. "Verses seven through nine." J. J. looks for cues, wonders if he should bow his head. Samuel reads.

For there is hope of a tree, if it be cut down, that it will sprout again, and that the tender branch thereof will not cease.

Though the root thereof may wax old in the earth, and the stock thereof die in the ground,

Yet through the scent of water it will bud, and bring forth boughs like a plant.

J. J. says, "You've got religion."

"Always had religion," Samuel says. "It just wasn't Ruby's." He goes into the garage, returns carrying the paper and a strip of duct tape. He attaches the scripture to the tree's trunk. He says to J. J., "Besides, that that I just did, that's not religion." He takes J. J.'s arm and they walk toward the house. "You're playing golf," Samuel says, "and you come to a par three with nothing but water between you and the green. It's two hundred and ten yards to the cup, which is hidden behind a trap, and you're going to have to nail the biggest two iron you've ever hit or use a three wood, a club you might as well burn for all the use you give it. You take a ball out of your bag—not a cut-up one, and it doesn't have to be brand-new—and you toss it in the water, far out as you can. It's a gift, a tithe. Now, your two iron will carry the water, no problem. You've acknowledged your debt to the gods." J. J. holds the screen door for his dad, and Samuel says, "That's not religion either."

Late evening, and Samuel and J. J. sit on the front porch of Samuel's house. It's wide enough kids could play kid-sized hockey or soccer inside its short retaining walls. The house's brick is plum-colored. Samuel swings on a glider, and J. J. sits on the top step. He's had his hand x-rayed, and it was negative for a break. The walnut-sized swelling is gone, but the red bruise has spread like floodwaters up three of his fingers and across the back of his hand. He pokes and tightens the skin, and his first knuckle hurts.

J. J. says to his dad, "What about the discoloration, does that mean anything?" He holds his hand so Samuel can see it.

Samuel glances over his reading glasses. His oxygen sits like a lapdog next to him. "You hurt your hand," he says. He stops the glider and says, "For a few days, just enjoy the various colors."

J. J. says, "It looks like blood under the skin."

They can see Flora in her yard. She's either planting for spring or cutting back for winter. Samuel says, "A couple of weeks ago

I went down and test-drove a Ford Ranger. Made me feel like a tall person." He indicates how he was sitting above the traffic around him.

"I can see that," J. J. says.

His father, who's about five-six, has put on weight, seems stumpier than J. J.'s ever seen him. Has a belly like the business end of a plunger.

Samuel says, "Question," like he's raised his hand.

"Shoot," J. J. says.

"Junior Junior, what are you doing here?"

"I came to see you."

"Why?"

"I wondered if I could help, if there was anything I could do."

"Like what?"

"Build you something." J. J.'s worked construction since he was sixteen. He rubs his sore hand. He squeezes it into a fist, and the pinkie hurts. He says, "Do you want me to go?"

Samuel's gliding slowly again. "You can stay till doomsday if you want. I never said you weren't good company." He lights a cigarette. His Camels and a Bic have been sitting on the arm of the glider. He blows smoke, says, "Is your divorce official?"

"It is," J. J. says.

"Sorry to hear that," Samuel says. He taps ash onto the porch. "I thought she was a good one."

"She was a good one."

"Better than that first lady."

"She was."

"Funny," Samuel says. "Ha ha funny, I mean."

J. J. says, "She was funny, and she had a great big heart." He cups his hands to show how big Lisa's heart is. "She'd do anything for anyone."

"Amen to that."

J. J. turns to look at his father, says, "Amen to that?"

"You see your kids often?" Samuel says.

J. J. says, "I'm a million-dollar dad."

"Be a five-million-dollar dad," Samuel says.

J. J. nods. If only he could stamp out what his heart feels, its bedrock hurt, its beefs and grievances.

Samuel says, "You don't really want to talk about it, do you?"

"I guess I don't," J. J. says. He does, but won't, not with Samuel, not with anyone. He'd only be vague and tell the lies we all tell, the face-savers. He'd only end up crying in his beer, talking about his loser status in this wide world.

When he turns around, Flora is crossing the lawn, carrying a box the size and shape of a Monopoly game. She's wearing jeans whose white stitching loops over itself like the pull string on a sack of feed.

Samuel stubs out his cigarette, gathers together his cigs, lighter, and oxygen, gets up, says, "She doesn't get in the house," and goes inside.

J. J. meets Flora at the bottom of the steps. "I had my boy order this for you," she says, and she's got the box open. Inside is a nylon wrap you can fill with hot or cold water. Flora shows him how. There's a rubber stopper that seals tight, but it has to be fitted exactly or it won't screw in and you'll get a drip. You feed straps through plastic, then it's Velcro to Velcro. Flora pulls the wrap around her thigh, stands back, and says, "It holds about two quarts, warm water. Just use the tap."

"So this is for the hamstring?" J. J. says.

She nods and undoes the wrap. J. J. holds the box for her, and she notices his hand. "What happened?" she says.

"From when I fell."

"My boy let Satan enter his physical body."

J. J. wants this to end, but doesn't know how to do that. He can't just walk away. His father would say, "Enough," and he'd raise his hands like he was about to push you off a cliff.

"My feeling is," Flora says, "that Satan can possess your body but not your soul. You give away your soul when you don't fight back, when you abdicate the throne God has given you. Your body, I mean, it is the temple of your spirit. It's in the scriptures." She folds the check into her pants pocket. "Satan tempted my boy with alcohol," she says. "He whispered in his ear, because my boy couldn't run, because my boy could barely walk as a result of what he'd done to his foot. Satan whispered in his ear, 'Just try this this one time. It'll be fun. You'll feel good.'"

J. J. says, "I'm sorry about your son."

Flora only stares at him. Then she says, "My boy did automatic writing. He'd sit at his desk, and the spirit would move his hand. He wrote down things that had to do with relatives he couldn't have met. They were dead. We'd never told him anything about these people, but he had the facts, facts he couldn't have known."

"I've got to go," J. J. says. He touches his chest, says, "My father's heart, you know. I worry about him."

Flora takes hold of J. J.'s wrist and says, "Let me just tell you this. Just one more thing." She slips her hand into J. J.'s good hand. "The Bible tells us Satan is the prince of the air. There is no place on earth for Satan to land, to set his foot unless we invite him." She lets go of J. J.

"I really am sorry," he says.

She says, "When my boy is running, everything is fine."

J. J. holds up the box and says, "Thank your son for this."

Flora follows him a couple of steps up the lawn, saying, "I go to the temple every day I can for my boy. When I'm not there, prayers are said for him for me."

J. J. wants to keep walking, but he doesn't. He can't even keep his back to her. He says, "My mother believed in the temple. It gave her great comfort."

Flora says, "Around here they say your mother was a wonderful person."

"She was," J. J. says.

"I know that my savior has forgiven me," Flora says. "I choose to rejoice. Every day you have to sit down with your grief. You spend time with it. You invite it into your home the way you would a guest. You talk to your grief."

J. J. turns to go in.

Flora is close. She touches his arm, says, "I know I'm keeping you, but just one more thing." She steps in even closer. "You know how little children go to people who smile. If you wear a frown, they won't come to you. My daughter noticed that. She's an artist. She also noticed that you never see a picture of Jesus smiling, so she painted one. She painted a portrait of a smiling Jesus for the children."

J. J. doesn't know what to say.

"You'll have to come over and see it," Flora says. "The original is in our foyer. We had prints made, and we sell them."

"Maybe sometime," J. J. says.

"They're prints," she says. "Not expensive. We want everyone to be able to afford one."

J. J. shrugs his no.

"Your father," Flora says, "he won't talk to me."

J. J. says, "He's that way," and now he can leave. He moves up the lawn, then climbs the steps and goes inside without looking back.

At 3 A.M., J. J. wakes. Something is wrong. This isn't Blondie-and-Dagwood-heard-a-noise-downstairs trouble. This isn't snore and grunt and out of bed to pee. This is someone with a bone to pick, and he's gotten into your head. This is knock-down-drag-out at the center of life.

J. J. finds his father in his bedroom slumped in a chair. He's been waking at night, short of breath, but this is something else. Four pillows, one on top of the other, are pushed up against the headboard. Samuel has pulled on pants, but not zipped them, and he's set out his shoes. They're slip-ons, tasseled, and the same color as the brick of the house. No shirt, no socks yet. "An ambulance is on the way," he says to J. J. "I want to be dressed." He gestures toward the closet.

J. J. selects a shirt, navy blue. Samuel gets into it, and J. J. buttons the shirt for his dad, even the collar. Samuel zips up his pants. "A cardigan," he says, and he points at his dresser. "White," he says. J. J. helps him into it. "Socks," Samuel says. J. J. hands him a pair, and Samuel turns them over in his hand, then flips them aside. His feet are swollen and cyanide blue. "No socks," he says. Samuel struggles to fit his feet into his shoes. He leans on J. J. to stand.

"Jacket?" J. J. says.

They agree on sport coat.

Samuel's sitting on a padded bench in the foyer when the paramedics arrive. He's hugging his oxygen, has a nitroglycerin pill under his tongue. He wants to walk out, maybe sit in the front seat, but the paramedics put him on a stretcher.

At the hospital, J. J. can't sit still, but doesn't want to wander far from the room where they've put his father. Samuel wasn't taken to Emergency, but to a way station off cardiology, a critical care step-down unit. The door's shut, and the doctor is talking to Samuel. J. J. stepped outside on his own. There's a computer in a recessed window next to the room. FOR STAFF USE ONLY.

Taped to the door frame is a hand-lettered sign. It says, FALL RISK. PLEASE BE QUIET. THANK YA! J. J. wonders if that's his father, and decides it must be left over. He keeps clenching, then opening his injured hand. The colors are kaleidoscopic. Ray Moss is Samuel's doctor, a cardiologist twenty years younger than his father, but Samuel's poker buddy, a reckless five-card-stud man. He carries himself like a soap opera doctor and talks like everything's an alibi.

Moss waves J. J. in, says in passing, "He may have had a stroke. We'll know pretty soon." J. J. is surprised at how good his father looks. A nurse is checking his lungs, moving her stethoscope like she's hunting water with a stick. He's got oxygen up his nose and is hardwired to a heart monitor, color-coded patches attached to his chest and inside his arms, but he's wearing a shit-eating grin and raising a hand to the room, saying something J. J. doesn't catch. Samuel's speech is slurred.

"What?" J. J. says.

"Rales," Samuel says. He gathers a hunk of his own hair between his thumb and middle finger, rubs the hairs together, and says, "Sounds like that."

The nurse rubs her hair together and says, "Perfect. That's right."

J. J. works a clump of his hair. It crackles.

"Fluid in the lungs," Samuel says. He gestures for the nurse to give him the stethoscope, and she does. Samuel hands it to J. J., says, "Listen."

J. J. hears the rales, the sound of hair rubbed between fingers, a crackling. He helps the nurse remove the pillows from the bed, and she punches a remote so Samuel is laid out flat. She zero-balances the bed. It's also a scale. Samuel weighs one seventy. She elevates his head, and the nurse and J. J. get the pillows back under him. She speaks loudly to Samuel, says, "I'm going to run an

I.V. push, Lasix." She turns his arm, examining the veins, says, "Nice big veins."

Samuel says, "That's the nicest thing I've heard in years."

She tightens a tourniquet around his upper arm and says, "I always get people on the first stick." She concentrates, aims, says, "The vein says we're in." She tapes the needle in place, starts the I.V., and says, "You've kept my record intact." She makes notes and then leaves, and J. J.'s father takes his hand and says, "At least it ain't ICU." His grip is weak. He asks J. J. to find him a Coke.

"Is Coke okay?" J. J. says. "I mean, can you have Coke?"

"There'll be a machine," Samuel says. "Or ask a nurse." His ears are pink, are backlit by lights on the headboard.

At the nurses station J. J. asks if his father can have a Coke. He's told it's no problem. He finds a machine down the hall and gets a can for himself and Samuel. He buys a *Time* magazine. Samuel's asleep when he gets back. J. J. can't read, can't really think. He sits by his father and sips his Coke. At one point a guy about twenty comes in and attaches a clip to Samuel's finger. A cord runs from the clip to another monitor.

"What's that?" J. J. says.

"Oxygen saturation." The machine reads 98. "That's good," the man says, and he's gone.

The word *stroke* scares J. J. It means bedridden, maybe a walker. Means one foot in the grave. Speech therapy. Words will be lost. The past will fade. Memories go. Samuel will forget Ruby's name. Maybe even J. J.'s.

About seven, Samuel opens his eyes and reaches for the Coke.

"I'll get ice," J. J. says.

Samuel nods. Now he's low. He's one indignity from crying.

J. J. pours Samuel's Coke over ice. He unwraps a straw and bends it for Samuel, and his dad sucks in a long drink. He cradles the cup next to his side.

J. J. says, "How do you feel?"

Samuel thinks long and deep on this. Then he says, "Used to be when I slept on my back I woke up with a hard-on."

On his way out of the hospital J. J. holds the door for two Mormon priests. They're sixteen-year-olds who are coming to give the sacrament to Latter-day Saints who've been hospitalized. J. J. knows how this goes. He did it before that day he abandoned the Mormon ship. Later Mormon elders will come and bless the sick. It's Sunday morning. The boys are wearing chinos. One's in cheap dress shoes that look like you'd use motor oil to spiff them up. The other kid's got on city sandals, light-brown socks showing through. His hair is shaved to the skull on the sides. Both of them look smug. Or maybe it's just teenager dull. J. J. can't decide. They're wearing white shirts and the kind of thin knit tie you find in thrift stores.

In the paper sack the boy in the cheap shoes is carrying are two silver trays. One has four rows of holes the boys will fill with thimble-sized plastic cups of water. The other tray is flat and solid and they'll fill it with small pieces of bread they've broken from a loaf they've brought.

They'll find a quiet room, and they'll bless the sacrament, the bread and the water. The kid in the cheap shoes will bow his head and say, "Oh God, the Eternal Father, we ask thee in the name of thy Son, Jesus Christ, to bless and sanctify this bread to the souls of all those who partake of it." J. J. has said those words. He knows the bread is to remind the members of the body of Jesus Christ. Latter-day Saints take the sacrament as a witness to God that they are willing to take upon themselves the name of God's son, Jesus Christ. They commit to live Christ's commandments and are promised that, if they do, "they may always have his spirit to be with them." This priest will know the prayer by heart.

The boy in the city sandals will bless the water. It will be given in remembrance of the blood of the Son. He'll read the prayer from a laminated card he carries in his wallet.

It's still early morning when J. J. parks in front of his dad's house. He's not ready to go in. He can see in his rearview mirror Flora standing on the corner of her lot, on the grass, at the top of the shallow knoll that runs to the sidewalk, and she's got her arms folded across her chest. She's ready for church. Her dress is the color of a peach. It's long, almost touches the grass. Flora's focused on the corner up the hill. Her son's not coming. He isn't going to turn that corner and, running like the wind, shift gears and coast down M Street.

Flora knows her boy knows how to run a downhill. It's second nature to him.

The photographer, he's on his porch, cigar lit, ready to take a picture, tripod, boxy camera, one of those capes hanging off the whole setup, like Brady shooting Civil War soldiers. But he isn't going to get a picture of Flora's son, if that's what he's here for, no shot of the boy's perfect stride, the foot plant exactly where it should be under knee and hip, the elbows set the way they should be set for the slant of M Street.

J. J. sits in his car.

He'll get a start on a ramp today. Stroke inevitably follows stroke—no? He'll build the ramp so it doubles back on itself and has a wide easy turn. The porch is high. He may have to widen doors inside the house. Some he'll take from their hinges. The hallway'll be a squeeze for a wheelchair. He's got to think about his dad's need for privacy. The man always shuts and locks the bathroom door. He keeps doors closed. Everything's dead-bolted. Maybe there's some kind of automatic setup J. J. can install, like they use in office buildings.

The photographer might as well put his camera away. He might as well swallow his cigar.

Flora keeps looking. Her grief is by her side.

The Egyptians built temples. They called the temple the House of Life. Their temple ordered their world. They taught us we can keep chaos at bay if we'll just keep thinking. Chaos is the result of the end of thinking. It was in the temple where the Egyptians thought, where they weighed and measured the enigmas.

There are so many ways to think. A world of possibilities. There's talk itself. Loquaciousness. There's reason. Logic. Math. Dance, that's a way of thinking. There's music. And photography. Photography's got its rhetoric, its choreography.

If we'll just put our mind to it, they say.

Thinking, King's X, time out, a way of saying Smoke 'em if you got 'em.

In the temple the Egyptians sang the creation song with the morning stars.

Flora, J. J., and the photographer, they could sing. They could hold hands and make a circle. Or alone. You can dance in a circle all by yourself. Workout videos, when they tell you to circle, they say, "If you don't have room, just circle in place." J. J., he could do that. Or Flora. Or the photographer.

But not today. Not this Sunday morning.

Flora, she can waltz, two-step, even fox-trot with her grief, but in the end she's going to have to eat it.

Think what we want, we all are.

THERE'S TOO MUCH NEWS

We moved to the woods of southern Ohio this summer, the backside of the Appalachians. Family phoned from Nevada, and we kept saying fall came, the leaves dropped, and we learned we had neighbors.

That's a good one, they said.

One or the other of us on the extension, we said, "Trees here, there, and everywhere, like in Red Riding Hood and slasher films. Like one of those gangster movies—you know, the place where the bad guys take the snitch to rub him out so no one's going to find the body for a hundred years."

Yeah? they said.

Before, we sent photos.

Gorgeous, they said of the colors.

Don't judge a book by its jacket, we said.

Take the deer hunt. Hill-jacks, five of them flushing whitetails along a draw and out of the woods, into open territory along Township Road 41, two of their buddies stationed in a field. Those two, they aimed, fired, and brought down a doe and a housewife who'd stepped into her backyard for a smoke, it being a fine sunny day and there being a baby inside. The numbnuts—clueless—were gutting the deer when the police arrived.

Some guy shotgunned his neighbor and dragged what was left of him onto the berm along Country Road 14. Another upstanding citizen stalked two hunters into a ravine and, using his own deer rifle, nailed them between the shoulder blades, a dispute having to do with a meth lab. Police found the men's dogs tracking along a dirt road. Report was, this was a repeat. Same thing happened last year.

Two nights ago, across from us, a hothead named Billy Fix beat up the woman he lived with. Paramedics, the paper said, found her in the garage, her car door open, keys in the ignition, radio on, engine off, a quilt thrown over her legs.

May, my wife, wasn't here for that. A couple of weeks ago, right around Thanksgiving, she said, "There's too much news," and she asked me to drive her to a place her psychiatrist recommended in West Virginia. Next day we drove down. Crossed the Ohio River at Pomeroy, took 62 along the river to Point Pleasant, and from there we followed a map they'd faxed us. On it were scribbled instructions about some place called Flat Iron, about a stone wishing well and drinking fountain at a crossroads where we'd have three choices (all of them eventually getting us to where we were going), followed closely by a narrow bridge where we'd have one choice. We pulled into a dirt-and-gravel parking lot, not sure we'd found the right place, no sign, but we'd followed directions to a T. The main building was a historical-looking two-story brick house, could easily have been your neighbor's. It was surrounded by a park. Cottages. I said, "I guess we made it," and May said, "By the skin of my chinny-chin-chin."

No phone calls for the first week, and afterward only every other day. Every third day would be most therapeutic. No visits for twenty-one days. Both mandatory commitments. For the sake of the patron. All parties had to agree or we might as well climb back in the car and drive home. I asked if twenty-one meant I could come on day twenty-one. "After day twenty-one," Dr. Clemens said. "It takes twenty-one days for wounds to heal." He capped his pen, said, "*After* is better."

May said, "Wounds?"

"It's a metaphor," Dr. Clemens said. "A factual one, though."

Patrons didn't ten-step or twelve-step. They springboarded. Here to here to here.

May's issues preceded us, a sweetheart teenage marriage, annulled. Darkness hatching guilt and crossbreeding into revenge. There was the usual stuff with her mother, only add a ton of intractability to each complaint. Loneliness, even at parties, particularly at family gatherings. Drinking, supposedly a thing of the past. Some OCD, spoon-stacking, toss rugs whose fringe must be splayed, chairs spotted up in rooms. Her feet, in conversation, set at eccentric angles.

May's father, a pharmacist, in order to teach her that life is chaos and must be tamed, painted object lessons on the walls of her bedroom. Imagine this, if you can: night, bedtime, May six or seven years old and already in her pajamas balked at brushing her teeth. That minute, he rolled onto the wall she faced when she slept a fresh coat of some kind of quick-dry flat-white paint. Half an hour later, he'd sketch in the story. He used a fold-up two-step step stool he kept in a corner of her room. First, one big square he subdivided into four smaller ones. Four frames. Frame one, a child—a girl—throwing a tantrum, refusing to brush her teeth. Frame two, the parents pleading, begging. Frame three, the child in bed, close-up detail of teeth decaying. Frame four, the child waking up, yawning, her teeth falling to the pillow. Always four frames, a cartoon panel, three-part cause followed by effect. To his way of thinking, how life itself spent its means.

Bizarre.

You agree?

In my book, the man had a lot of explaining to do when he reached the Pearly Gates. There was no excuse for it.

May was an only child.

We'd been married seven years, and this was the third time she'd gone for therapy. First time, I said, "You're in a bad marriage?"

She hugged me, said, "We'll see."

Second time I said, "Do we need to talk?"

"It's not us," she said. "Case closed. You and me, we're fine." She hugged me, said, "I've fallen overboard and need this lifesaver."

Our place in Ohio was built on top of a hill. I worked out of the house, my office three floors up, high enough I had an aerial view of the street, of the houses on the other side. From where I sat, now that it was fall and those leaves had dropped, I could see 33, the highway I'd eventually take to where May was. At night, one, two, three a.m., I watched taillights climb the steep grade, seem to hesitate, then fall out of sight. I heard the truckers down-gear. You know how sound travels when it's late.

The woman directly across from us—her name was Lee— owned the house. Billy Fix moved in with her after we arrived. A couple of days before the incident, at work in my office, I watched Lee's daughter draw a stick figure on a cemented area of the front yard. She used chalk and drew a girl, hair yellow as healthy corn, in pigtails, hot-red face, blue shirt and skirt, two different shades, that skirt a perfect isosceles triangle. She added hiking boots and colored them brown. A thunderstorm banged through that night and washed it away. Big, booming storms, they came and went and sounded like war here. On the lawn, snug to the cement, was a basketball standard, one of those whose base you fill with water. I sat here the day Billy Fix wrenched it together, watched him and Lee tossing a ball at it, neither of them any good. They aimed their shots, didn't know how to drop their weight to their legs. His style was jerky, and Lee followed suit, like they might have been jabbing at deadly snakes hanging from tree limbs.

Billy Fix, wouldn't his name be something like that? Can't you hear his friends calling him Fix or Always, as in Always in a Fix. It's an alias you'd have taken if you'd have ridden with Jesse James.

Lee's driveway swung downhill to a two-door garage under the house. Behind it, a ravine ran to the woods. Where the lawn met the trees, mostly birch, some sycamores, bright red-leafed bushes grew in a hedge. Every night, the same five deer came up the hollow, crossed the yard and the street, hoofed it by our place, and headed for the woods behind us. One, a doe, was white, an albino. Some mornings, I spotted them nesting at the edge of the trees, curled in sleep, like stones.

They told me at the C&E down on Richland Avenue that the streets where we lived used to be deer trails. The builders simply took what was already laid out. When you drove up into the neighborhood late, the moon did a three-sixty on you, met you where you least expected it to be.

About ten that night, the yelling started. I shut off the floor lamp at my shoulder. Could see some of what was happening from where I sat. Billy Fix kept coming out through the garage and ending up in the yard, huffing cold air. A movement-sensitive light'd come on, and he'd be pacing, one hand to his head, like bad acting. He yanked his truck into gear and slammed out of the garage.

Sat in the cab, smoking. He killed the engine. He kicked a basketball into the trees. Mostly he walked around, passed in and out of shadows, like he was on a set of cards I was flicking to make him move. Once the light popped on, caught the deer in the open, and they retreated up the ravine. There was this sense I was watching it all through wicker.

It was because of the newspaper I know it was Lee the paramedics put on a gurney. Not that I couldn't have guessed. A cop drove away with her daughter. Billy was long gone. His truck, you saw it in daylight, first thing you noticed was it had a ram hood ornament, and across the front of the hood, above the grill, stuck to a hard plastic were the kind of reflector letters you see on mailboxes, the ones that catch light. These said, GET READY PEOPLE.

"The nuns are getting better," May said on the phone.

I said, "They're springboarding, are they?"

She said, "Would you announce, when you leave here, you've been sprungboarded?"

"Makes me think of leapfrog," I said.

She said, "Nuns at leapfrog. Picture them on the lawn after a game of croquet."

Nuns in rehab. We'd already done most of the jokes. It was day seventeen, and we'd talked every other day since the first week. You tried to sneak in an extra call and they had records they referred you to. "Sir," they said, and then gave you the dates you'd talked. Begging wouldn't have fazed them. I need her would have been embarrassing and meant nothing to them.

Nuns rehabiting. Under-the-cover nuns. I had said one night, "Nuns in rehab, it's, what? Redundant?" Not quite the word.

And May had said, "Tautological."

Now I said, "How can you tell they're on the improve?"

"They changed their habits," she said.

I said, "They stopped flying so high."

"Have you noticed," May said, "everything's a competition?"

Our joking? I thought, and I felt guilty, the way you feel when you bad-mouthed some slowpoke on the highway or in a grocery aisle and then you realized they're syndromed in some way. I said, "It's how the world does its business."

"The orange juice I drank this morning," she said, "it claims it has *as much calcium as milk*."

"They're bragging so you'll drink it. For your bones. They're betting on you wanting something other than wholesome trustworthy milk. Variety is the spice of life."

"Why all the bragging?"

"If it's true, it ain't bragging."

"Seriously?"

I said, "Tell me seriously about the nuns."

"They smoke like a house afire. You see this group of them moving along like a choo-choo train, a cloud of smoke drifting up and away puff puff puff."

"So you're saying they aren't there to quit smoking?"

"Their sins are bigger. Weightier."

"The weightiest," I said. Thinking, Sins?

"See," May said. "What I said about competition?"

"But they're getting better otherwise."

"It seems so."

Our doorbell rang. It was after eight, dark, and someone had crossed the lawn where I couldn't see them. I said to May, "There's someone at the door."

"I heard it," she said.

"They'll go away," I said.

"Answer it," she said. "It'll be an adventure."

I hesitated. Thought, Adventure? Not dressed for one.

She said, "Go. Go. You can do it."

I picked up the cordless, which I hated, its sounds from deep space, its nastiness about its battery, its sudden way of quitting on me. I punched it on, said, "You there?"

"I'm here," May said.

I said, "I switched phones."

"Hurry," she said. "You don't want to miss them. Make believe it's Beggar's Night. Have whoever it is do a trick." Her talking like she was an actual person was in my ear, fully dressed, wearing shoes, a hat, gloves, hair combed.

"You wouldn't make them do a trick," I said.

"I'm not there. You are."

I flicked on the porch light and pulled open the door, felt it resist and then suck the air from the entryway. A boy—seven, maybe eight—stood there. A woman was behind him and off to the side, like this was a stage, her in the wings. She could have been a child or she could have been forty. Their clothes were thrift-store simple. She said to the boy, "Say it."

"What's going on?" May said in my ear.

"Say it," the mother said. The boy looked at her, then me.

I said, "Can I help you?" The phone was tilted so May could hear. I wanted to tell her it was trick-or-treat all right, only in reverse. The boy was holding a plastic see-through zip-lock bag. Inside it, a Snickers and a Mars bar, both of them king-sized. I said, "Do you want food?"

"Say it," the woman said to the boy.

I heard May say, "What's up?"

The woman said, "Do you want to buy a candy bar for a dollar?"

I said, "No," then got in my pants pocket, saying, "Wait." I fished out a five-dollar bill and handed it to them.

"Say it," the woman said to the boy.

He said, "Thank you," and started to hand me a candy bar.

"No," I said. "Have a good night."

I watched through the screen until they crossed the grass toward our neighbor's, all the time May saying, "What's going on?" until I filled her in. I said, "I'm turning out the lights."

Before I hung up, I told her about Billy Fix and Lee, about the cop and Lee's daughter, and May said, "What did you do?"

What had I done? That night I had turned out the light for a better look. Telling her that seemed dumb. Saying I didn't really know what happened was rationalizing at best, disingenuous at worst. Describing where I sat in relation to what was going on was hairsplitting.

She said, "Even in Ohio there are numbers you could call."

Late afternoon, the day before Lee came home from the hospital—I'd heard talk about a broken arm, skull fracture, some kind of trouble with her vision—Billy Fix parked in Lee's driveway, and Billy and a boy unloaded bags of peat, wood chips, and sand. They piled flat rocks along the path to the front door. They'd spent the morning raking leaves into the gutter in front of the house, building a hedge of them the length of the yard, knee-deep, thick and high enough a big dog could get lost in the piles. Couple hours later a city truck rolled by and sucked them from the gutter. The kid, Billy guiding him, climbed a maple and cut limbs womb worms had infested. Checker at the C&E told me if you let them go they kill the tree. Billy and the kid cleared and mulched the flower beds and sculpted a new one along both sides of the walkway. Dry-stacked the edges. They planted bulbs. Billy'd take a break, sit on the grass, light up, and the boy'd shoot hoops. Like Billy, he had no game, everything about him was short-circuited. He pounded his dribble into the driveway, as if the basketball wouldn't return if he didn't wail on it. If he didn't airball his outside shot, he banged it off the backboard and ended up chasing the ball down the hill and into the ravine. Nine times out of ten he tripped when he drove for a layup. Billy crossed his legs and smoked. I thought about shutting down the cost analysis I was doing and going over. Maybe offering to help. Take a minute and show the kid how you use your fingers when you dribble.

You wonder about people like Billy Fix, if they have thoughts, or if they can just sit and be.

Fix and the kid drove away and returned with an ornate cement pedestal and a gazing ball, this one the shimmering blue of a rock-singer's dress. They cleared an oval in the grass, placed the pedestal dead center in it, topped it with the ball. Disco in the front yard. They unloaded an iron bench—wood slats for the seat—and positioned it at a slant to the ball in the oval. Billy Fix sat a cloth doll at one end, tall as a five-year-old. Looked like it was dressed for a party.

Next morning, Billy was alone in the yard, a do-rag on his head and stripped to his Marlon Brando T-shirt, when a black Buick pulled up and a woman helped Lee out of the passenger's side. I could see her daughter in the back seat. She wasn't budging. Billy could have been the yardboy the way he stood by. He dropped his shovel, took a couple of steps toward the women, then stopped. Lit up. I don't think anyone had said anything.

The woman returned to the car and walked Lee's daughter into the house. No real coaxing, just being there, like a sidecar.

Billy got in his truck and drove west toward the highway.

Then later, after dark, I heard him stop in front. Didn't hear his truck door open or shut. Imagined Billy in the cab, smoking, wearing his own skin inside out. The woman's car was still there, and from where I was there were no lights on inside the house.

I shut down the computer—realized I hadn't turned any lights on in my own place—and descended to the kitchen, hitting switches as I walked. I hadn't eaten since nine in the morning, hadn't showered, was still in my sweats from my morning run. I dumped tomato soup in a pan, thinned it with milk, and, stirring slowly, dialed May. Three transfers after someone picked up, I was told she was out on the grounds. I said, "It's night there, isn't it?" Trying to orient myself to which way it was the sun dragged itself across the heavens. Could it still be up where May was? No. East to west is how it goes. The East Coast beats the West Coast, is alive and kicking first.

"We're well lighted, sir," a man said. He said his name was Alan, that he was an attendant.

I said, "Is it cold?"

"Unseasonably warm," he said. "Still sixty. I'll tell her you phoned, sir."

May wasn't allowed to make calls. I never did get the rationale behind that commitment. Easy enough to bill us, no? And there's always collect.

I heard Billy's truck sputter and choke itself off. Its door opened and shut. I reached our living room, my soup on a tray, in time to see him pivot on a cigarette and start up the walkway to Lee's. Then the motion-sensitive light winked on. He stepped sideways, his sharp shadow on the grass. Next he walked right in.

An hour later, I reported all this to May, and she said, "I guess yard work is what they do here instead of roses."

Me on the highway, I was listening to local talk radio the next morning debate whether or not Jesus would have carried a handgun. I was driving 33 north to a truck stop I like. Great hash browns. Even greater omelets. On the radio one lady—she sounded elderly, maybe in her seventies—said Jesus didn't need to. She said, "He used a cat-o'-nine-tails to chase the money changers out of the temple."

"He's God almighty," some guy said. "What would God almighty need a gun for?"

The host interrupted the talk to say he'd gotten a fax telling him he'd been wrong earlier. Jesus, the fax said, wasn't a fisherman. He was a fisher of men.

"Got a joke for you," one guy said.

The host said, "If it's clean, we're ready."

Guy said, "I'm sitting in my house, all the windows open. Know why?"

"Can't guess," host said.

Guy said, "It's the deer hunt. I can hear the bullets whizzing by and I don't want them busting my windows."

"That's your punch line?"

"That's it."

Next guy wanted to discuss sex, how to spice things up in the bedroom. Said, "I'm afraid I see things in magazines and see them in the movies."

Host cut him off.

The truck stop looked like a crew hauled in three houses, bolted them together, and aluminum-sided the hybrid they'd jerry-rigged. What I liked about it, what got me to stop the first time, was there was a sign in one of the three big windows that fronted the place. It said EAT. Neon. Red letters two feet high. EAT. Can you get to the point quicker? Not in my book.

So, first time by, I ate.

Along the sill at the bottom of the windows were potted cactuses, a mixed bag, fat, bent and browned, all of them scraggly. Inside there were two rows of tables that looked like they belonged outside a Taco Bell in the West, the kind of booths you take your fast food to on a day the sun is shining. There were three round dining sets, hand-me-downs and leftovers, you'd think, from moves, from relatives who'd gotten a bonus and purchased new furniture. No lunch counter.

Now I sat in a corner and didn't realize Billy Fix was here until he was standing next to me. I'd already ordered. He said, "I see you up there at your place."

"It's where I do my work," I said.

He nodded and took out a pack of cigarettes, said, "You mind?" He withdrew a cigarette. Pocketed his pack.

"I do," I said.

"How about I take a load off?" he said.

"If you want."

He settled in across from me, fingering his cigarette. A part of me wondered if he'd tailed me. If I'd have looked, would I have seen his truck in my rearview mirror? GET READY PEOPLE backward. He said, "Not that it's any of my business, but what is it you do up there all day?"

I said, "It's where my computer is."

He tapped his cigarette on the table, kinked its tip. "I see you watching me," he said.

"I'm thinking," I said. "I sit where I do by the window to think. It helps me. Sometimes I notice. But what I'm doing is solving a problem in my head."

"You want to know, I drive cab in the winter," Billy Fix said. "The rest of the year I'm out at Lake Snowden in a camper I own. No heat." He waved the woman who ran the restaurant over, and she brought him a cup of coffee, a tin creamer. She said, "You eating, Billy?" Everyone called her Bea.

He shook her off, said to me, "It gets cold and I start staying at Lee's. She's not much for the camper herself."

I said, "That your boy with you the other day?"

"My sister's."

I said, "Billy, I don't want to be rude but is there something you want?"

My food arrived, Bea saying, "Excuse me," asking if I'd like ketchup and finding some when I said yes. Billy studied his bent cigarette, said, "Lee, she started smoking because of the cat." He leaned back. "I found it at the lake," he said. "You can bet someone dumped it out. Said to it, *Good luck, puss.*"

I said, "A campground's the kind of place they do that."

"The smoke kept it off Lee's lap," he said. "See, the cat'd come sashaying toward her, and she'd light up."

I said, "I'm going to eat."

"You go ahead." Billy stayed put.

"I'm not spying on you," I said.

He said, "I understand you."

"I'm up there, and I'm mulling things over."

"You said."

I dove into my omelet.

"People say I can draw anything," he said. He lit that cigarette, blowing smoke away from me, saying, "I'm certified by Disney, one of those courses they used to offer around the country through the mail. Only trouble I have is filling in the colors, which could be one of those disorders like when you can't read words."

"So you're an artist?"

"I'm anything but."

I was swiping jam on toast and didn't answer.

He wiggled his fingers in the air, left hand, said, "I use only chopsticks to eat with. Learned that from a real artist. From a man who can call himself an artist. It's for the dexterity."

I had a mouth full. Just nodded.

"You and your wife have children?" he said.

"We don't."

"Brothers?" he said.

I didn't answer him.

"You don't have to answer," he said. He tapped ash into an empty cup on a table next to us. Now I was just looking at him. He'd turned sideways to me, was resting his pointy elbows on his knees. "You know how you make a Doberman mean," he said. Bea signaled him to get rid of the cigarette. He took a last drag, crushed it. I'd stopped chewing. "You put gunpowder in its food. See, like that omelet you're eating. You could sprinkle some in while you're cooking, and it swells up the dog's brain." He curled his hands like he was holding a dog's brain. Then he expanded the space. "Dog'll get crazy. Tear your dick off, you come close."

I sat back.

"I offend you?" he said. "I apologize." He raised his hands, innocent from his head to his toes.

I said, "Billy, you're ruining my breakfast."

"Am I?" he said. He said, "Let me pay for it."

"Just leave."

"You got any pals?" he said. "You go in a bar, and you sit by yourself? Like in here? You come and go by yourself? My bet is you never bought another man a drink. You never said to a buddy, 'What's yours? Bourbon or whiskey?'"

"If you say so." Truth was, I hadn't. Fix was right.

"My second bet is you spent your life sitting around talking to women," he said. "Like Lee. You could probably talk to her all day. Am I right?"

I set my fork aside and got up.

"Your wife is gone, sir," Billy said. "Life is one inch one way or the other."

I said, "Whatever you say," and tossed a tip on the table.

He picked up a dollar of it, snapped the bill, said, "You understand me, don't you?" It would have been clear to an astronaut on the moon I didn't. Had no idea to his point. Felt like I was in a tough-guy skit. This was improv, and I was clueless, couldn't come up with any lines. He said, "Thing is, you wouldn't want to live near a mad dog."

At the C&E, stocking up for May's return, wheeling a cart, I almost sideswiped the woman and the boy who'd come to the door. The boy turned out to be a girl. Her bad haircut did terrible things to her face. They were in the candy aisle, and I was after chocolate, dark with almonds, May's guilty pleasure. They were two-fisting candy bars into a handbasket.

Met them again at the registers. No basket with them. The girl was checking out a display of Picnic Barbie, Barbie in red-checkerboard pedal pushers, a denim vest, her hair platinum. She was outfitted for a picnic, tiny six-pack of Coca-Cola, tiny Coca-Cola cooler, tiny Coca-Cola Frisbee. The girl's mother, in front of her, stared straight out the front windows, one Milky Way in her hand. The girl turned the Barbie box over. There were cutouts on the back—a tablecloth, mustard, ketchup, four meals on their plates.

I unloaded, and the mother paid, the girl slipping behind her, drifting toward the doors. I bought a Barbie, a joke I'd pass along to May. Grown-ups playing dolls. We'd go on our own picnic, take Barbie along.

The woman and the girl, walking, were halfway up the hill that wound me into our neighborhood. I downshifted and slowed, a car coming the other way, and I watched the girl fetch candy bar after candy bar from her pockets. It was marvelous to see. It was art. She was ambidextrous, as herky-jerky and agile as the squirrels we fed. It was genius. I swerved, then caught her in the side mirror. More candy bars—one, I swear, plucked from behind her ear.

You'd have forked over good money to see it.

Day twenty-one, and I was on 33 again, going south. Plan was, I'd drive down the night before May checked herself out and find somewhere to stay. Be there bright and early next day. She'd decided she'd had enough. Her wounds had healed. Maybe we'd drive over to D.C. for a week. We hadn't been yet. Or New York. Why not? We moved here and we got in the mail this packet of information that told us what we were in driving distance of. D.C., Great Lakes, Chicago in one day, New York City itself, beaches that had been only names to us.

Still on the Ohio side of the Ohio River, I swirled the car through an *S* in the highway, emerged out of some woods, and saw more yard art than you imagine anyone could stand to see in one lifetime. There was a house off the road, quarter of a mile up a slope of lawn, huddled in the trees. From the front porch to the road, nothing but yard art. Black plow horses in red harnesses. A unicorn. Lawn jockeys. A guy in a sombrero taking a siesta. Your ducks and your geese. Cardinals big as dogs. And a pair of hands. These cupped hands, upright, painted bubble-gum pink. Huge.

"What's with the hands?" I said.

The owner'd come out when I pulled up the lane to his place. The hands were taller than I was.

He said, "Four hundred pounds each. They're solid concrete."

I shoved a pair. Might as well have been pushing on a building.

"You won't be budging them," he said. "You want to buy a set, I got a forklift out to the back."

As if my car could have dealt with a pair of four-hundred-pound concrete hands. I shook my head. "Who does buy them?" I said.

"People got different names for them," he said. "Some call them prayer hands. Some say they're blessing hands." He cupped his own, acting like he was pouring water from them. "People say they're for baptizing."

I said, "But four hundred pounds."

"Certainly."

Temptation was to ship a pair to the family out there in Nevada. Maybe my brother and his wife. Have them arrive out of the blue. Big truck pulls up in front, backs in, beep beep beep. Two guys unload a crate. Provide a courtesy crowbar. More family gathers. Here come the neighbors. The delivery guys hang around, curious.

I bought a cactus. He had one he'd spray-painted green. Its base was the color of the desert, and in what was supposed to be sand there was a cow's head molded out of the cement, a skull, just bones, like you see in the movies.

I said, "It's a saguaro."

"I knew that," he said.

We were cross-armed, carrying it to my car. It weighed close to a hundred pounds. No way would it fit in the trunk with the luggage, so we set it in the back seat. Propped it up with some pillows I kept in the trunk. Tell you the truth, I had in mind Billy and Lee. I'd haul it over myself, show him I had something to offer in the manhood department. May'd be there, and the four of us, Billy and Lee arm in arm, Lee completely herself again, we'd move the cactus around the front yard, stand back, stroke our chins. In the end, Billy'd decide where. We'd let him.

Next morning, there I was. Indian summer. Great day.

I was about to the front door when I saw the nuns drive by. A van load, one of them at the wheel, another one riding shotgun, smoking, twisting in her seat to light the cigarette of a nun who was leaning into the flame.

Had they springboarded—been sprung, going home—or was it just a day out?

May'd know.

Inside, they told me she was on the grounds, probably had walked to the lake. She had a favorite spot, they said. Alan gave me another map. Muddy paths led me through the trees, most of them bare, scraggly, and sad-looking, but also enough conifers to keep the place pretty. Cones and leaves thick on the ground. Where there was grass it was spongy. There were gaps you couldn't have gotten through except on foot. Deep dark sunless areas. I followed those wooden signs, distance and directional arrows carved into them. I crossed a footbridge, a grove opened up, and I could see May. Beyond her, in the shallows, was a white bird the size of a child. It was mirrored in the water, so when it stepped, its reflection led it. It dipped for whatever it was it was feeding on.

There was so much to tell May. The Barbie doll, for one. Maybe we could hunt down the girl and her mother, give it as a gift. There was the cactus riding in the back seat. How was I going to explain that? It'd be fun trying. Welcome home, I'd say.

Didn't want to forget the magic with the candy bars. I'd demonstrate, pull one from behind my own ear. It'd just take some practice. Was a simple matter of misdirection. Everyone understands how you do it.

I was about to call out May's name, and she did something with her hands. Raised them, then slowly brought them to her chest. It could have been a prayer or exasperation or a celebration or utter despair. Was something she took to her heart. Was a gesture I knew I'd see over and over in the days ahead.

Whatever, she got the bird's attention.

It looked up at us, May and me, May not aware yet that I was behind her.

Had to tell her about the big letters, the neon-red EAT. But not Fix and the café, except to let her know he's an artist. I had no plan to tell May about the gunpowder and the Doberman.

If I did, she'd ask, What did you say?

THE 12-INCH DOG

Doc rubs the bump in the palm of my hand, wags my bird finger, and says, "Dupuytren's contracture." The bump's the size and hardness of a kidney bean and is centered inside the top of the V of the M of my life line.

I'm working on how to describe Doc to my wife Patty. She'll ask me to. His face looks like it was torn apart and then mended under gunfire. His stiff ears poke out and are stamped crude as buried treasure coins. They're padlocks. The eyes belong on a parrot. He's got porcupine hair and junkyard teeth.

"It hurt much?" he says and grinds down on the bump. Says, "When I do that?"

I say, "Oh, my, no."

Doc's sitting below me on a padded stool, and there's a 12-inch dog in the corner. Sucker's no taller than a footstool and is black as ink-bottle ink and hairy as hell. Doc says, "Dupuytren's is common enough. We see it in men more than women." He walk-scoots away on the stool, pushes off, zips to an instrument tray, and comes up with a Milk-Bone he hook-shots at the dog. The dog's toenails clatter on the linoleum. He gets purchase, leaps and snags the Milk-Bone a clean foot and a half off the ground and lands soft as popcorn, no click, no clatter. Doc says to me, "Worst-case scenario is amputation." He's braced himself against scary-looking machinery, heavy-duty black casings, curled and loopy hoses, knobby dials, a sci-fi prop. All we need is test tubes. We need beakers heating over Bunsen burners. "It's a joke," he says. "Only kidding. Tales told out of school."

The dog crunches its treat, and I wring my sick hand. "There was a pope who had Dupuytren's," Doc says. "He had Dupuytren's of the little and ring finger. Only his was severe. Like this." Doc raises his hand, the little and ring finger bent down and into his palm, and says, "It changed how the Pope does his blessing. It's supposed to be all four fingers straight up, hand wide open, flat." Doc clenches his hand, flexes it. "Now his blessing is the one you see on TV, him in the Popemobile, little and ring finger down, index and bird left standing."

The dog stops licking crumbs and grins fiercely. He thinks this is funny.

Doc says, "Do you know if your dad's got Dupuytren's?"

"My dad's gone," I say. "He passed away."

I try to picture my dad's hands. He's dead five years now, and I see him in his casket holding hands with himself, his nails color- less, his fingers waxy and orange. A man who never drank or smoked, who respected God in the way he dressed and talked and sat and swept a floor, who double-checked every fact he built his private and business world on, my father toppled over at work— the man was a Realtor, as honest as his thirty-eight-inch sleeves— fell over one morning, dead, someone said, before he hit the ground. I was fifteen, still in high school. Aneurysm. Like a blow- out, they said. I say to Doc, "What do I do?"

"Not a thing to do right now." He helps me up, shaking the hand he's just pronounced diseased, and opens the examining room door. He says, "I've got me a motto. If it ain't broke, don't fix it. If it hurts, whirlpool it. Someday maybe corticosteroid if it gets worse, which it may or may not."

I say, "I'm not yet twenty-one, Doc."

He gives a nurse my chart, pats my shoulder, and says, "God, to not yet be twenty-one."

I'll tell Patty he was as kind as a hangnail. She needs to keep in mind I'm a man of wit and humor. Got my own motto: When in doubt, go for the joke. Doc walks toward the front desk. "You're in your prime," he says and enters his office. The dog swings alongside his foot as disturbing as a loose shoelace.

At home I describe Doc to Patty and explain Dupuytren's contracture and the Pope and the 12-inch dog. I'm thinking she's getting a kick out of how I'm telling all of it. I chomp my teeth together so she'll hear the crunch the dog made as it snagged the Milk-Bone in midair. "Landed soft as a sponge," I say. I tug at my ears and my hair when I tell her about Doc's ears and his bristly crew cut. "Hair like a razorback hog," I say. "Teeth like Judgment Day." I inform her he was as sympathetic as a paper cut.

Hot water in a kettle breathes on our stove. Patty's mute. She's poured us both a cup of instant Maxwell House.

I show her how Dupuytren's changed the way the Pope blesses us. I run through the names of the fingers, teach Patty what my grandma taught me, *Tommeltot, Slikkepot*—I illustrate how you use *Slikkepot* to slick the pot clean—*Langemand, Bullenbrand, Lillepeter Spillemand.* I point at the trim on the stereo so she'll see how black the dog was, and I fetch our footstool and hold it so she'll see how tall. We're at the kitchen table, sunlight on us the way it should be for newlyweds, which is what we are.

Patty gets up, tops my cup off, says, "Fibber," and slips around behind me, saying, "Liar, liar, pants on fire." She bangs the kettle onto its burner.

"Go ahead and touch it," I say, standing up, sidestepping the footstool, opening and closing my hand. I'm spinning around and around, actually getting dizzy. At my back, she's half a step ahead of me, juggling her coffee and sort of square dancing. I say, "It's big as a grape, almost, and hard, hard as a dirt clod."

"I'll touch that," she says, "when the cow jumps over the moon, when the spoon runs away with the dish." She puts her cup on the counter.

I turn around, and she's ahead of me at staying behind me, quick, like she's me in a clothing-store mirror. I say, "What's wrong? What's going on here?" Patty is flying off in one direction, and I seem to have been knocked in the other. Patty and me, we're married six months this week is all. We've done this ass-backward dance into the family room, and on top of the TV is the 11-by-17 photo we displayed at our reception. Patty's in her wedding dress, and the photographer has pooled its train in a circle around her feet. She looks like she's stepping out of a white hole. The background's mostly burgundy but swirled like marble. There's an insert of her face in an oval. She's white as a rose and has twisted and fantailed her black hair like cake. We got through her honeymoon cystitis together. Our moms took care of it. Patty, she's just turned twenty, but up to this very minute she hasn't shown signs of the lowlife stupidity that runs in her family. I barely graduated from high school, and she didn't, just quit, but neither of us is dumb. I've got a brain you couldn't fit in a grocery sack, although education itself just makes me fidget. Sitting in rows. Those tight-ass desks binding you taut as a package. Patty's nervy and owns a tongue you don't want to have to deal with. Right now, I got me work sandblasting headstones, a job that isn't going to quit on me, death being up there with taxes, as they say. Working day in and day out puts me in touch with human nature, a subject worth anyone's time and study, and I can talk both your ears off.

Patty says, "Plenty is wrong." She sounds like her mother, like her dad. Without warning, life is now yes and no. I can't get her to look at me. She says, "You're a wolf in sheep's clothing."

Stupid as the floor I'm standing on I look at what I'm wearing, even turn inside out and study a corner of my shirttail.

"You went to the doctor for some queer sickness, for some homo problem you got," she says. Patty's still behind me, is like some beast in a forest. What she is saying is stuffing its furry self down my throat and hunting my heart like the 12-inch dog soaring through the air after its treat. In my chest, it's barking. I'm a boxer who's been toyed with for seven rounds and now the uppercuts hurt like fence posts to the ribs, like ramrods. I kick throw rugs across the hardwood I laid myself, and they hide in corners and under furniture. I can't catch up to her.

She says, "Your homosexual friend called." Up to this minute Larry's been *our* friend, and we didn't call him homosexual, gay, or otherwise. Larry was Larry. Larry was Spanky, was part of our gang. The three of us went from kindergarten and on into high school arm in arm. Larry recommended Doc.

I push the bump, and my bird finger wobbles.

"Larry boy," Patty says. "Cute little Spanky."

I say, "Go ahead and put your finger on it. It's under the skin." I offer her my hand. I say, "If you don't believe me, just touch it. You can. It won't infect you. It's Dupuytren's contracture." Feeling I've got here is I'm on the lam. I'm the guy who walked away from a work detail at the state pen, and I'm asking the pretty stranger whose home I've stumbled upon under a clump of trees in the foothills to believe that I'm the hero of this story. I'm the mug who's been wrongly accused, tried and convicted. My face is all over the evening news. Bulletins keep coming in. Reports say I'm armed and dangerous, but I'm not. If you were listening to your radio, there'd be a news break about me. But God's truth—and the right people know this—is I didn't do what it is I'm charged with. All the evidence is circumstantial, won't hold up. I say to Patty, "Every bit of what I'm saying is true."

She says, "Spanky wondered how it went at the doctor's. Spanky wondered if you're okay. Spanky wondered if you found out exactly what's wrong. Spanky wanted to talk to you and only you."

I go to the phone on the wall and punch in Doc's number.

"You didn't tell me you were going to a doctor," she says.

Phone's ringing.

Patty says, "Milksop bungholer."

Milksop bungholer?

The cord's too tight. I can't stretch the phone across the room to her.

She says, "Cur."

Time warp here. We've stepped off a roof and tumbled into another century. "Listen," I say. I want her to *hear* what Doc has to say.

Patty says, "Spanky's come a-courting, and it's not Patty he wants. I see how he looks at me. He looks at me how a woman sizes up another woman who's in her way. And his hair, the way it drops onto his forehead like musical notes. Tell me he has perfect toes, and I'll puke on your shoes." She's stopped tailing me and is crying, tears bigger than light bulbs. She's wearing bright red strappy sandals, and they shine like apples. She sobs out that she's not naive. She knows about *bi* and swinging both ways.

There's something going on here that isn't being said. At some point, while I was gone, Patty shook out a rug and came up with a crime. I didn't tell her I was going to the doctor because I didn't want to trouble her until I had something to say. I was thinking cancer, was sure it'd spread to its farthest lethal point.

I wedge the phone to my ear and hold out my Dupuytren's contracture, offering Patty my hand's delinquent life. I say, "What I've said is true."

She says, "Not the dog part. They wouldn't allow it."

I squeeze my hand shut.

She says, "Fool me once, shame on you. Fool me twice, shame on me."

No one's answering at Doc's. It's after hours. Finally, a recording picks up and tells me Doc's partner is on call. There's a phone number for emergencies. "Maybe we can catch him," I say, "before he actually leaves," and I jangle the truck keys. "He might be doing reports or something." Patty won't come.

So, for an hour, it's me accounting for a crime I didn't know was a crime. Patty, she's sealed up, has burrowed into her hair. I might as well shoot arrows at a locomotive. This is a one-man game of tetherball. She sags from the sofa to the window seat to the La-Z-Boy her folks passed on to us. I talk her into a Coke and spike it with rum, and I yak on and on, describe the 12-inch dog in the air, compare him to Russian acrobats. I redescribe Doc's face. This time his hook-shaped question-mark ears are dried fruit. His eyes are a fish's. He's got hair like a toothbrush, teeth like a shark's.

Larry phones, and Patty won't talk or even sit in the same room with his voice. She answered, didn't say a word, just flipped the receiver onto the sofa. I picked it up and reached for her, but she dodged me and went out back. Larry thinks the story about the Pope and the dog and my hand is funny. He asks if we're going to be around tonight because he wants to cook for us, red snappers a cousin passed on to him. I don't tell Larry about Patty. I just say we're going downtown. "Come over later," I say.

It's warm, and in the backyard I sit next to Patty on our redwood deck. In the park behind our place, beyond our cinderblock fence, the Krishnas are setting up for their annual Festival of India. You can see their temple from our place. At dusk they'll slay the evil demon Ravanna. The striped tops of the multicolored wedding tents they've pitched stand out against the hazy blue mountains to the west. Someone's playing rock music. Japanese honeysuckle's sweet perfume fills the air. We planted it and three trees across the back of the yard. We've put in ivy and kudzu against Patty's mother's advice. It takes me another half an hour, but I talk Patty into tacos. She drives—wants, she says, to be able to pull over and get out if her spirit moves her. My ten-year-old Toyota short-bed is arthritic. It knocks us along the streets, somehow enlarging the tombstone of silence that rides between me and Patty.

She pulls into the drive-thru, but cars are wrapped twice around the Taco Bell, so we go in and then take our food to one of the outside tables. They're round metal, painted white, and they've got umbrellas stuck in the middle. We face the side of a laundromat. Up a back street, alongside a bowling alley, comes Doc's 12-inch dog. He's got something in his teeth and is moving like he's walking on blistered toes and legs brittle as twigs. "That's Doc's dog," I say. The dog sees me, spits out the trash he's hauling, and trots over to us.

"Watch this," I say to Patty, and I toss a corn chip.

The dog gathers himself, leaps, and nails it in the air. He comes down chomping.

"I suppose you see this as some kind of evidence," Patty says.

I spread flat part of a taco shell and salad on a wrapper and invite the dog over. Every part on him goes up, his ears, his tail, his muzzle. This dog's ribs show. I coax him to me, and he attacks the taco. It's not Doc's dog, I don't think, although, thumping down the last bite of taco, he's grinning as fiercely as Doc's did.

Patty says, "The dog here proves nothing."

Proof of what? Who's trying to prove anything? Is this an interrogation? A cross-examination? Go ahead, I think, put a 150-watt bulb in my face. Grill me. Truth's on my side. Where's the rolling pin?

One day you're sitting over the comics, got yourself a sweet-tasting sticky cinnamon roll, you're licking your fingers, and you rub a bump in the palm of your hand, think, Cancer, decay and death, slow and miserable, cell by cell. Your pal gives you his doctor's number because you don't want to upset your pretty just-turned-twenty wife, and you find out you've got some pope's disease, which you're not to worry about, but while you're gone a time machine lands on the lawn behind your newly purchased tract house, and eighteenth-century patriarchs in high collars and beaver hats hop out, chase down, kidnap, and replace the lady you've hooked yourself to forever. They drag your wife kicking and screaming back in time. In her place is a harebrained look-alike who's using words like *milksop*, *bungholer*, and *cur*. There's no song for what's happened here. Even country's ignored this subject. No one's written a how-to book.

I'm not yet twenty-one. Patty's just turned twenty. Isn't there a grace period? Aren't we underage? Don't we get a couple of years during which the good times roll?

Patty has gotten down on her knees and is petting the dog. She lets it sip from her Coke, then offers what's left of her enchilada. "This dog's nothing but skin and bone," she says. She runs her hand along its spine. The dog's got one winky eye and is wearing a collar but not tags. Patty says, "We've got to help it." She runs a finger around the inside of the collar, says, "Too tight."

"We'll call Doc," I say.

At the house, I dial the emergency number Doc's recording gives me, and I get an answering service. I explain to the lady that it's not medical, that it's about Doc's dog. I need Doc, not the partner. They'll have the doctor call me, if they can reach the doctor.

Patty's set two bowls out, and the dog is lapping water from one of them. She tells me to check the newspaper.

No ad for a 12-inch dog.

It's too late to call the pound. Patty says, "This dog's been gone a long time."

"Anything on the collar?" I say.

"Just that it's too small. He's outgrown it." She unhooks the collar and tosses it in the trash. You can see where it's dug into the dog's neck. It's cut him, worn away the fur. It's left scabs.

"I saw that dog in Doc's office," I say.

Patty cracks two eggs. She's put a fry pan on and starts whipping the eggs in a bowl. She tells me to get a tub of cottage cheese.

Larry comes through the door, no knock—we're that close— but something's screwy. His hair's up like our mothers wore theirs in high school. He pats it and says, "What do you think?" He's wearing a white shirt and a red bow tie. If it spun at his throat I wouldn't be surprised.

Patty, stirring the eggs and cottage cheese in the hot fry pan, is leading the dog into the backyard.

"It's a feather bob," Larry says, gently stroking the hairdo. He explains his niece who's studying at a beauty college couldn't find anyone for the hairdo part of her state exam, so he volunteered. "We had a great time," Larry says. "Don't you love the smell of a permanent?" He reaches for his bow tie. Now he'll spin it. He tightens the tips. He's got some Polaroids his niece took. "I'll get one enlarged and framed for you," he says.

I look out the back window and see Patty headed around the side of the house. The dog's trotting along at her side. The fry pan and an empty bowl sit on the lawn.

"What's going on?" Larry says.

Before I can answer, the phone rings. It's not Doc, but Doc's wife instead. I tell her we found Doc's dog.

"We don't have a dog," she says.

Patty, on the sidewalk, passes in front of the house. She's gone out the side gate and is headed toward the strip mall around the corner. The dog's not taking its eyes off her.

I say to Doc's wife, "The one he keeps at the office."

"They wouldn't allow that."

Larry has gone out and is calling Patty. She stops, picks up the dog in one arm, and flips Larry off. He yells, "It's me, Spanky," and tugs at his hair like he could jerk one string and undo it all.

I tell Doc's wife about the Dupuytren's contracture, about the black dog, the Milk-Bone, how the dog nabs it in midair. She tells me to call Doc in the morning. She knows nothing about a dog. She says, "Wouldn't surprise me, to tell you the truth."

Larry comes in puzzled, says, "What? Am I the other woman?" and I have to explain that he is, that he and I are lovers and I went to the doctor for AIDS. "Fool Patty once," I say, "shame on you. Fool her twice, shame on her."

"Jesus," Larry says. He picks at his hair. It's slopped to the left. His niece passed her exam, but I can't see how. The hairdo's not holding up. Larry says, "God. Are you serious?"

"Let's clear the air," I say.

We jog up the street and turn in the mall parking lot just as Patty comes out of Pets R Us. She bought a Hawaiian-print leash and matching collar. She's got dog food and shiny steel dog bowls. She's carrying a box of dog treats. There's no place for her to hide, and she's too loaded down to run. She hands me dog food, bag and box, and a video attached to a Frisbee. It's the Frisbee Dogs Training Video. Satisfaction is guaranteed. It includes a doggie diploma. Larry takes the bowls. He's been talking since we turned the corner and almost ran into Patty, saying, "Patty, Patty, Patty. You're wrong. This man's straight as a yardstick." Larry's hair keeps falling off to one side. He tightens his bow tie and says, "It's Spanky." He's gotten in close, the way he does, and is talking two inches from Patty's ear, and she won't look at him. She won't look at me. "It's come to this," Larry says. He puts one of the bowls on his head, steps directly in front of Patty, frowns, and twirls the other bowl clumsily on one finger. It wobbles once or twice, then stalls.

She's fighting a smile, and the dog is growling under its breath.

He gives her a bowl and adjusts the one on his head. Larry calypsos, arms swinging across his chest. He's wearing flaps, and they add their own flippity-flop beat. He sings something about *these bones, these bones, these dry bones.* The feather bob, fighting for its life, has lifted the silver bowl up and the bowl's about to fall. Larry snaps it off before I can steady it.

Patty leads us into a park. A band called Krishnautix is playing, and there are booths, vegetarian food, gifts, all under the wedding tents. Ravanna, the ten-headed demon, stands in an open field. They've made it out of crepe paper. Krishna warriors have gathered around the demon.

Larry flattens out his hair and says to Patty, "Spanky. Remember me?"

I'm holding my wrist and flapping my hand in front of her, saying, "My dad might have had Dupuytren's."

Patty stops us.

Larry says, "Pat—"

"Shut up," she says.

There isn't much light, and Ravanna the demon has begun to move. Someone is shaking the effigy. Lord Rama lights a flaming arrow, aims, and hits the beast in the shoulder. Ravanna catches on fire. Two more flaming arrows and the demon is blazing in the twilight. It's like watching a building burn, sad and thrilling. Out in the street, just in case, city fire trucks wait.

Patty says to us, "Watch this," and she flips her hand over. The dog sits up. She runs through hand signals, and the dog rolls over, plays dead, begs, and shakes. The dog looks like an old tire that's learned to do tricks.

I say to her, "How did you know how to do that?" and I repeat one of the commands she used. I snap my fingers. The dog ignores me.

She says, "Never you mind." It's her mother talking, it's her grandmother. It's that wench from eighteenth-century England. Patty shows me the form she used to order tags for the dog. They'll come in the mail. She's calling him Rocky.

Larry says, "He's too smart, and trained. He must be somebody's."

"Finders keepers," Patty says.

"Losers weepers," Larry says.

In the open field, the Hare Krishnas dance around the demon Ravanna. All ten of its heads are smoldering.

Rocky heels good as a show dog all the way home, is a wad of gum stuck to Patty's left ankle. Me and her and Larry, we walk together, like we used to, like pals, and Patty tells me and Larry she's going to sell her eggs. She called about it while I was at Doc's. The university's medical school pays for the procedure, and they give you three thousand dollars. She says, "You know you're born with all the eggs you're going to have. I thought they were talking about an egg, one egg, but they're going to take all my eggs."

What about us? I'm thinking, Kids? We don't need three thousand dollars.

All her eggs? Has she gotten her facts right?

She says, "Mom called. She's got a yeast infection all through her body. She can't eat flour or anything like that for a month." She points at her stomach and says, "I don't want a little baby in here."

We put the Frisbee video in, and Larry washes his hair in the kitchen sink. The Frisbee Dog Training Video is Veterinarian Approved. We're supposed to get a physical before we start, and so is Rocky. The music is workout rap. Dogs are catching Frisbees five, six, eight feet off the ground. A collie bounces off its owner's back, flips in the air, and chomps down on a Frisbee. The star of the show is Whirlin' Wizard, the World Champion. We learn about the best Frisbees. The polyethylene surfaces won't cut Rocky's mouth.

Kids, I'm thinking. I had in mind a couple, a boy I'd name Chad and a girl Patty could name. There are things I'd like to pass along. My old man was no genius, but he fixed things, and he knew how to sell. He was always cheerfully saying, "That's the why-to, where-to, and how-to." I'd slip a golf club in Chad's hands when the kid was in the crib, and he'd grow up to make us all rich. What is there to golf? I've never played, but my dad did, and I see the fatsoes on TV. They stroll from tee to tee, some skinny old guy the color of tobacco doing the real work, lugging their clubs for them, The fatsoes pinch grass and test the wind, whack at the ball, get their bellies behind their swings and pick up a hundred grand for finishing third or fourth. Start the kid early enough and he'll kick butt, buy us a home, help me retire in my forties. He'll spring surprises on me and Patty, an RV long as a block, a Jeep, one of those Desert Storm Hummers.

Whirlin' Wizard's owner is teaching us how to grip the Frisbee. You place your fingers along the bottom of the disk, index finger—*slikkepot*—curled along the rim. He makes a neat throw, and Whirlin' Wizard runs it down.

Patty has set up Rocky's bowl in a corner of the kitchen. She hammered a nail in a door frame, and his leash is hanging there. She's adjusted his new cloth collar. Larry, drinking iced tea, a towel swirled around the top of his head like our mothers do, says, "Pinochle?"

"We don't play cards here anymore," Patty says. She runs her finger around the inside of Rocky's collar.

"Pinochle isn't cards," Larry says.

She says, "Cards is cards."

I pour a glass of tea and step outside. The Krishna tents are coming down. There is ash in the air. No cards, I think. *No Cards?* No kids, no cards. Since when? I sip my tea. There are gaps between gate and fence I'll need to cover so Rocky can't get out. I'll check the lawn and flower beds for glass.

Back inside, I see the video is teaching us about throws. There are four types. You've got to keep the Frisbee flat.

Patty's on the phone. She listens, shaking her head, then says, "If this is your dog, you didn't take care of him. This dog's skinny and weak as a Kleenex."

I crouch down in front of Rocky, twist my hand over, and say, "Sit." He knows he's already sitting. I try the flip throw, watching the video while I do it. I snap the Frisbee at Rocky, do it just right, my wrist coming down hard. Rocky watches it bounce at his feet. No way is this dog going to do anything for me. He's got his DNA. I've got mine.

"Your dog have a white tip on its tail?" Patty says.

Tricky of her. Someone's cropped Rocky's tail. It pokes from his body like a tab, and there isn't any white on it.

"Yours does?" Patty says.

Her mother'd do that. Sucker the guy. They should have their own quiz show.

She says, "This one doesn't."

I add, "Damn right."

Patty hands the phone to me, saying, "That rum sucker's not getting this dog."

I look at the phone.

"Talk to him," she says. "He wants to talk to you."

I say, "Doc?" into the phone. On the video is the word TAKE. Whirlin' Wizard's owner kneels in front of the dog, stuffs a Frisbee in his own mouth, and signals for the dog to take it. Whirlin' Wizard jumps up and plucks it free.

"How's the hand?" Doc says.

I thumb the bump, say, "Okay."

"You found my dog?"

"We found a dog. Doesn't sound like it's yours."

"It's black."

"Not as black as yours."

"Did it have a collar on?"

"Not like the one in your office had."

I can hear Doc on the line, but he's not talking. Rocky is sitting by Patty, who is at the table with Larry. I say, "Doc?"

"Your hand's okay?" he says.

"Sure."

"That bump's not growing?"

"No." I thumb it again.

"Not getting any harder?"

"No."

"Your finger's not curling down at all."

"No."

"You sure?"

I hang up. The video has begun a lesson called PRAISE. It tells us this is a key to our getting Rocky to like the Frisbee.

Larry is combing his hair, the towel around his shoulders. He pulls hair straight back like wet grass. He's kicked off his flaps. "No red snappers," he says. "But I could whip us up something to eat. We can always do potluck."

"We ate," Patty says.

"Patty," Larry says. He takes her hand as sweetly as any sweetheart has ever taken his sweetheart's hand, and he says, "Are we okay here?"

"I've led with my chin one too many times," she says. She bends over and Rocky waltzes into her arms. She hefts him to her lap.

I say, "Led with your chin?"

She holds Rocky's ears up and says, "I won't be bamboozled."

Larry points at me, says, "Him Tarzan." He points at himself. "Me Jane," he says. His hair actually has furrows in it. What he's said puzzles him. He pats at his hair with a towel and begins recombing it, saying, "No, no, no. That's not right. That came out wrong." He points at me with the comb. "Him healthy man with manly appetites. Him want woman. Me want man."

Patty rests her head on top of Rocky's.

Larry stands up, folds the towel, downs his iced tea, and starts for the front door. "I'll make my exit gracefully," he says. On his way out, he says, "*L'chayim.*"

The video is ending, is showing us dogs doing unimaginable catches. We've been warned that our Frisbee dog is an athlete. We need to keep plenty of water on hand.

The sun just dropped below the west mountains, and Rocky is exploring the backyard. I tried some basic tosses, but the dog acted like I had offended him. Doc called back, and I talked through my nose, pretended he had the wrong number. "No one here found a dog," I said.

Silence. He was stonewalling.

I said, "You're barking up the wrong tree."

Patty sits next to me. She's got wine, and I'm working on a fresh glass of iced tea. Rocky studies our landscaping, like he's naming bushes and trees, the shrubs, like he's worried about their health. Honeysuckle rolls over us. Patty's mother has warned us about the kudzu. It'll bust out your windows and destroy your house. It's a killer.

"These are our salad days," Patty says.

By her side, on the redwood deck, is a jar we've stuffed with cut flowers. There are some roses, red streaked with white. They look a little like Larry's bow tie. Our ivy is already climbing the fence.

"We doing all right?" I say. I'm fiddling with my Dupuytren's contracture.

Rocky rolls in the grass, trying to rub the top of his head.

"Only time will tell," Patty says.

Quoting who? I wonder. Her mother? Her grandmother? That Victorian lady who's taken up housekeeping in one corner of her mind?

She says, "No more peace at any price."

I offer her my hand, palm up. "Want to feel it?" I say.

She says, "I trust you."

"About your eggs," I say.

The sun has dropped below the mountains, and the hills are darkening, shadows creeping in thick as water. It's as if someone has set up a row of floodlights behind the mountains. We're on our side, waiting for the show. Rocky, as black as the night will be, quicksteps over and sits at Patty's feet. He freezes in place.

I say, "Your eggs?"

CAUTION: MEN IN TREES

Bobby Book wonders what the fuss over Bugsy Siegel is all about. Why the movies? Why the full-page spreads in newspapers, five columns deep plus photos? Bobby's father, Lewis, met Siegel. His shop did the sheet metal work for Siegel when he built the Flamingo in '46.

Lewis, who's in his seventies, lives with Bobby and his wife. He has a cottage out by their pool where he sleeps till four every afternoon, when he gets up, has one drink, Old Grand-Dad neat in his tumbler from the Mirage, hops on his left leg for half a minute and on his right leg for another half a minute, flips upside down and stands on his head, handsprings right side up, lifts free weights, gleaming eight-pounders, swims twenty-five laps in the pool, and then gathers together the bits and pieces of his threadbare yet still lethal body and heads for Caesar's Palace on The Strip. There he hobnobs with the old crowd, with men named Shoetree Walker, Walleyed Eddie, Rose-in-the-Pocket Jackson, old retired Twenty-one dealers who dealt when you were expected to hijack enough silver dollars your first go-round to make up for the shit-ass pay, men who knew how to tuck chips up their sleeves and inside their waistbands, who in the 1990s in Las Vegas, Nevada, still call women "dolls." "Hey," they say when they greet you, when they glad-hand you and cheek-kiss your wife, "win a dolly for your dolly."

You ask him, and Lewis will tell this story about meeting Bugsy Siegel. He goes to Siegel's hotel door when they're finishing up the duct work at the Flamingo, and a thug opens it. Guy's big as Jumbo. Siegel is behind him, pit-a-patting on his feet, jitterbugging to see who it is. Jumbo takes one step toward Lewis and clogs up the doorway. He raises his hands, saying, "Don't talk," and looks up and down the hall. He picks Lewis up and sets him aside. Behind Jumbo, Bugsy Siegel is antsy, is saying, "It's not the guy at the door you worry about. It's the guy behind the guy at the door."

Benjamin Siegel, Bugsy, Murder Inc.—the Bug, they called him behind his back—was, according to Lewis, dumb as an anchor.

"Why Bugsy Siegel?" Bobby asks his wife, Polly. They saw *Bugsy* at the fourplex one night, and now she's rented the video, and Alice, their daughter, is coming over to see it. Alice is as deaf as mahogany.

"The man's handsome as a movie star," Polly says.

"The man," Bobby says, "is rotting in a grave, is full of bullet holes. Those baby blue eyes, the teeth he paid thousands for, they blew them away." Bobby marks a circle on his face, his middle finger moving from his forehead to his ear to his chin to his other ear and back to his forehead. He feels like he's somehow genuflecting here. "Whoever did it shot a perfect circle on Bugsy's face," Bobby says.

Polly pretends to swoon.

Bobby says, "He killed people."

Bobby's seen the porous gray photographs in the newspaper, and he can't figure out the attraction. Bugsy Siegel looks cheesy in photos. He had a short upper lip and was droopy-eyed.

"It's more than good looks," Polly says. "America is changing. The country's different."

She tells Bobby they've killed off the real Superman. The Lone Ranger's on kiddie shows, fat and lumpy in dippy Kmart reading glasses. She explains that the U.S.A. is a desperate country full of sad sacks. She tells Bobby your everyday mom and pop are in need of heroes.

Bobby says, "Of all people, why Bugsy Siegel?"

Bobby's question is part of the irritability he's gagging on. He's spent the last two hours with Archie Cohen out on Tropicana and The Strip. Cohen's a man Bobby'd not met until this afternoon. Archie Cohen dressed like a mobster in a movie, like Bugsy Siegel. He wore an eggshell-white suit, double-breasted, and he kept sticking his pasty, flat Napoleonic right hand between lapel and lapel and running it slowly up and down his potbelly. His pants hung forties baggy in the knee and cuff. His mint-green tie matched the stripe in his shirt and the handkerchief in his coat pocket. The tie's design, slightly-run-amok Art Deco, swirled and floated like the germ world you see under microscopes. Archie wore two-tone, white-on-brown Oxfords. He looked like china dishes, like a wedding pattern.

Bobby listened to Archie Cohen, chewed on his own tongue, and thought about but didn't ask, "Are you packing? Carrying a roscoe? Do you rub people out?"

They stood on the hard-as-brick caliche under a 14-by-48-foot billboard. Archie Cohen slicked back his already slicked-back hair and pointed at the sign. Its base stood thirty feet above them. Bobby had sold Archie's casino the space. The sign showed three playing cards fanned out, the jack of hearts on top. There were stacks of chips on each side of the cards, and big red lettering said SINGLE DECK '21.' Along the bottom, five-foot letters read 10 X ODDS FREE DRINKS FREE INTERTAINMENT.

"*In?*" Archie said. "*I . . . n . . . in* tertainment?" Archie had a nose like a Chinese fortune cookie, and he kept tapping it, as if the fortune itself had gotten hung up on its way out of a nostril.

Bobby, waxing poetic and under the tug of a waning moon, will tell you he is not a rat in the labyrinth of a midlife crisis. He'll get downright mad. He sells outdoor advertising, owns the damn company, and is the best at what he does. "BB"—short for Best Buy—is what they call him. Bobby "BB" Book. He plays five or six rounds of golf a week, and he can eat Mexican any night he wants and not end up with gas in the bilge. He doesn't wear glasses of any kind, even for reading. Sure, he turned fifty last week, and he's got two boys of his own and enough grandkids for him to mess up their names. Alice is his one daughter, and she *is* deaf— *profoundly*, they say—but what does that have to do with anything? She's married and happy as a songbird.

For BB's big five-O party, the family stuck a sign on the front door. QUIET, it said, WAKE IN PROGRESS. Bobby's daughter-in-law Cindy tied black armbands on everyone and handed out name tags that said MOURNER. Polly swirled black streamers across doorways and from overhead lights to lamps, and she tacked black balloons to the walls and ceiling. It all came together like a spiderweb. She ordered black icing for the cake. Lewis, on his way out of the house heading for Caesar's, wearing what Bobby thought must be a zoot suit, had given him a one-hundred-dollar bill he'd folded into a one-inch square turtle. He patted his son's shoulder and said, "Live it up. You're not getting younger."

Bill Jacobs and Vern Isakson, two neighbors, sneaked over during the day and hung thrift-shop jumpsuits in Bobby's closet, his choice of colors—red, green, blue, gray, and a light brown. At the party, they led BB, the family, and guests into the bedroom, slid open the closet doors, and sang a song about the jumpsuit fairy. The jumpsuit fairy knows when you've been forty-nine. The jumpsuit fairy knows when you turn fifty. The jumpsuit fairy knows when you've been good and bad. No one could goad Bobby into pulling one of the suits on. "Be a sport," Polly said. No way was Bobby going to be a sport. Bert, one of the salesmen from work, gave Bobby a box of condoms FOR FIFTY AND OVER. Big letters said ONE YEAR'S SUPPLY. Inside was one condom. BB's son rigged the smoke alarm to go off when Polly carried in Bobby's cake.

The night of the party Bobby, still up after he and Polly had cleaned away the dishes, nibbling on cake, alone, slipped into the light-brown jumpsuit and stood in front of a full-length mirror in the hall. He thought he'd shit on the carpet. He set aside his plate of cake. His lampblack hair paled and fell out, and his father's face nudged his out of the way. Bobby jerked around, quick as you would to throw open a shower curtain when you get that creepy feeling someone is hiding in the tub. No Lewis behind him. No Lewis looking over BB's shoulder. What Bobby saw in the mirror was not funny. He was one of those linen dinner napkins folded in that fancy restaurant way, then unfolded, and no way did Bobby know how to get it back the way it was. He felt like one of Polly's sad-sack Americans listening to an old song he loved, but some New Age star was singing it differently, more slowly, and Bobby was for the first time actually hearing the words, and they were dumb words, real dumb.

Archie Cohen, living with a surgeon's precision the advertisement of his life, had stood on the caliche, the temperature 110 degrees, his clothes the same color as the ground, saying peevishly, "*I...n. In. Intertainment.*"

An easy mistake to make, Bobby thought. You pay fools, you get stupidity. Most of the company's sign painters had third-grade educations.

"It makes me look bad," Archie said. He moved his hand up and down between the lapels of his suit. "That kind of error in what we call the decorum of life makes us look like some kind of lowbrow casino." He tapped his nose.

They could have handled this by phone, but Archie wanted Bobby out here. He wanted the president of the company on the job site. Archie had called Bobby at home, had said, "Mr. Book, the sign you sold us, we've got a problem. You'll want to see it."

"What's wrong?" Bobby had said, thinking, How did this jerk get my number?

Cohen's casino *was* a lowbrow casino, a wanna-be jammed into the cracks left between the big hotels. Bobby didn't need any grief from this twit.

"Meet me," Archie said. "In one hour, out by the sign."

So Bobby did. And here it was, INTERTAINMENT in gold, the five-foot-high letters on a blue background.

"It hurts us beyond words to be associated with this kind of thing," Archie said to Bobby, and Archie put on his sunglasses. Archie touched where his heart was, seemed about to cry, and said, "Right here. It hurts us where we live."

Bobby told him it would be taken care of by five.

"You mean, of course," Archie said, and he took off the glasses, wiped them with his mint-green handkerchief, "you mean by five today."

They walked to their cars. Archie's was a Jaguar, white body, white interior. If only, Bobby thought, you could still buy those four-inch-wide whitewalls. Archie Cohen said to Bobby, "It's like *end zone*, you know?"

"What's like *end zone*?" Bobby said, and he thought, God, I'm shoe-horning myself into my straight-man shoes, yanking firm to my forehead my straight-man cap, pulling on my straight-man coat.

"In-tertainment," Archie said. "End zone. Dopes say *in zone*. You hear it and you don't want to do business with this kind of ignorant person. You hear it on the TV, from the sports people. They're paid to know better, you know. They appear as if they don't know their business. We don't want to give that impression, do we? End zone, not *in zone*." Archie opened his car door and put on his sunglasses. He tapped his nose. He said, "What did the knife say to the other knife?"

Bobby said, "You've got a good point?" Refusing to step into his straight-man pants.

"Not bad."

"But not what the knife said?"

"Nope."

On with the straight-man pants. "What," Bobby said, "did the knife say to the other knife?"

Archie tugged his coat straight and said, "Looking mighty sharp today."

Back at the shop, Bobby hassled the art director, sat in the man's office until he saw two painters load up a truck and head out to the sign. BB had written *entertainment* on a three-by-five card, underlined the *e*. He phoned Archie and said, "A crew's on its way."

Archie said, "Mr. Book, sir, do you know how to make son-of-a-bitch stew?"

Jesus, Bobby thought. Jokes. What is this, the mob's sicced its comedian on me? The mob keeps a Bob Hope on its payroll? I need a break here. Give me one.

"You use everything you can of the steer—the hair, the horns, the heart, brains, kidneys," Archie said. "But what you can't leave out, what makes son-of-the-bitch stew son-of-the-bitch stew, is the gut. If it don't have the guts, it isn't son-of-the-bitch stew."

Bobby said, "Your sign will be done by five."

So it's Archie Cohen in Bobby's face in the heat, and now it's Bugsy Siegel in his family room. From where he sits at the dinner table, Bobby can see city workers in the front yard. They're trimming trees away from power lines. Three crews are working the street. A wiry kid, roped to the trunk of the biggest tree in Bobby's yard, swings from limb to limb, tying off branches, then cutting them, and an older guy, maybe Bobby's age, waits on the ground and feeds branches into a mulcher. His sideburns look like roman numerals. He has long hair pulled into a ponytail and wears a long beard. The sixties left him behind. They've set up their sign in the street. It's orange, shaped like a stop sign, and says CAUTION: MEN IN TREES.

Bobby's on the phone, making one last bid to a tool company for a string of billboards along the Boulder Highway. The tool people want an extra month free. Bobby won't budge on the offer he's made. "This deal's on its feet and it's walking out the door," he says. He retracts the pen he's been figuring with and pokes at the peace sign he tattooed on himself one night thirty years ago. He hadn't been drunk, just bored. It's on his left hand, covering that web of skin between his thumb and forefinger. Over the years it's gotten blurry. Growing up in Vegas, Bobby hadn't given a rat's ass about the peace movement. He'd just done whatever he had to do to keep his own ass out of Vietnam.

How about a billboard on The Strip for the money they're paying? the tool company wants to know.

"You're burying me," Bobby "Best Buy" Book says. "You're

shoving your hand into my pocket, filching dollar bills and taking a squeeze at my balls while you're at this form of highway robbery."

Alice, coming through the back door, walks her twins in and signs, "Hi, Dad." The twins sign it, too. They're girls, just turned five. They're barefoot, two grimy look-alike faces and four identical feet, twenty exactly-the-same sooty toes. Alice holds up their shoes she's had tucked under her arm and shrugs, *What's a mother to do?* The girls have on mismatched tops and bottoms, and together, standing so they seem stuck to each other by Popsicle juice, they come across as toss pillows. They've smeared chocolate around their lips. Bobby gives them a baby-wave, his fingers tapping out a message on a telegraph.

"Where's Mom?" Alice signs.

Bobby nods toward the family room where Polly is setting up to watch *Bugsy.* Dinner itself will be catch-what-you-can. Alice herds the twins into the hallway.

Outside, the kid in the tree rides the limbs. He cuts one free and lowers it to the lawn, then lopes up the trunk to a higher branch. The old guy below him shoves the limb in the mulcher, and it's eaten up. The kid lassoes a branch, swings through the tree, and ties it off at three different angles.

Polly walks by, shows Bobby *Bugsy* and a Tupperware bowl full of popcorn, and says, "Sure you don't want to watch with us? We can wait."

Bobby, hand covering the phone's mouthpiece, says, "Go ahead." The tool company is one concession from saying yes.

The twins, behind Polly, follow her, tag along like pull toys with bad wheels, with tires bumpy and out of alignment. Each girl walks like she has a flat. One has a sprig of hair that sprouts up and left. The other's sprig shoots up and right. Alice has put red barrettes in their hair, and they're wearing Minnie Mouse sunglasses.

Bobby adds one sign to the tool company's contract, and they accept. In the kitchen, he runs into his father. Lewis has been swimming and has wrapped a Turkish towel around his waist. It hangs as matter-of-factly as a short skirt. What's left of his hair lies in threads above his ears and down the back of his neck. He's carrying his tumbler of Old Grand-Dad. "What, why so glum?" he says to Bobby.

Before Bobby can answer, the twins tumble through the door and skid across the linoleum. They act like they're tipsy. They've got balloons for Grandpa. Lewis sets his drink on the counter, takes the balloons, scoops one twin up, and says, "So, whose little girl are you?"

She says, "Alice's," and signs it. Neither twin is deaf, but when you talk to them they zero in on your face as if you're a gadget. Lewis puts her down. The other twin wiggles her hands at him. She says, "Lift up. Up up up and away." Lewis cradles her so she's sitting in the crook of his arm.

"Why don't you come with me tonight?" he says to Bobby. He is twisting the twins' balloons into animals. The squeaking hurts Bobby's teeth. "We can play some poker, you and me and my pals. Nothing but five-card draw, no ad-libbing, which is stuff this little girl could do, but simple pleasures for us old guys whose memories have gone south to Mexico." He has to put the twin down to finish the balloons. They study him like he's God. "Maybe we get feeling frisky and play some Hold'em," Lewis says. "Us old guys, we're not bad company. We've got stories to tell. Bugsy Siegel put a gun in my ear. Did you want to know why he did that?" Lewis has twisted the balloons into teddy bears. He holds them out for the girls.

They sign something to each other. They're clumsy at it, but are as serious as they are over candy. Then suddenly they're slapping and bonking each other as if the Three Stooges have taken over their bodies. One ends up crying. The other one is red-faced and snot-nosed. Lewis coaxes them toward the family room, keeps the balloon bears just out of reach, then gives each girl one, and they disappear around a corner, sucked toward the love of their mother, weeping, small people in a big world that has just upset them for no reason at all.

"You know how that goes," Bobby says to Lewis. "I'd like to come, but I've got to meet a man about a job."

"Which is crazy, that you've got to meet a man about a job at this time in the day. Or at any time—why are you still selling space? As if you're not the one who owns the company business," Lewis says. He looks to where the twins have gone. They're howling. Lewis says to Bobby, "You walk from here to there like you've got hold of your own tail." He shrugs, picks up his drink, and finishes the Old Grand-Dad, then rinses out his tumbler. Suddenly, no sound from the twins. Lewis has lifted his weights, hopped up and down, and his ride will be here in half an hour. "This is not sneaking around, is it?" Lewis says.

Bobby says, "I don't sneak around."

"You'd be a jerk to. I raised you to remember putting yourself in other people's shoes." Lewis walks past Bobby, headed for his cottage. He stops at the sliding glass door, says, "It's never just you and a woman in bed scratching some itch you have in common. You involve people."

Back at the dinner table, Bobby gathers together his notes on the tool company. He hears *Bugsy* start. Outside, the tree crew is cleaning up for the day. They've worked late. The guy Bobby's age is loading equipment into their city truck, and the kid is raking the lawn. His shirt, unbuttoned, flaps loosely against his thighs. He's working over the grass like it's marble he's got to polish. He's not missing a twig, and now the old guy, a gasoline pack strapped to his shoulders, has picked up a blower and is blasting wood chips off the driveway and into a pile he can scoop into a bag.

Bobby stops in the doorway to the family room. Bugsy Siegel has just gotten to Hollywood, and George Raft has picked him up in a great-looking old car. The real Siegel, when he went to California, brought his wife and children with him. They came with mob money and a certain degree of mystery. No glamour. Bobby watches Polly sign to Alice what Alice can't lip-read. Alice feeds the twins popcorn, one kernel at a time. You don't give them fruit. They'll scream. She sees Bobby and wipes her hands on a paper napkin, then signs, "Watch the movie with us?"

"That's not the real story," he says. He signs this while he talks.

Polly says, "This story's better." Alice turns to her, and Polly signs what she said. Polly says to Bobby, "Bugsy Siegel was good-looking, but he wasn't Warren Beatty." She's signing for Alice.

Alice signs, "No one looks like Warren Beatty."

"I don't know," Bobby says. "They say the real Bugsy was a lady-killer."

"Bad," Polly says. "Real bad." She signs Bobby's joke for Alice. Alice holds her nose. She's saying, P-U.

Bobby tells them Lewis says the Flamingo was a big success from the night it opened. All the stars from Hollywood flew in. He signs while he talks, and Polly pauses the video. He tells them the nightclub entertainers begged to perform and then dropped their pay at the tables. The Flamingo pulled in more than three hundred thousand dollars the first night. It didn't rain when the Flamingo opened, and it wasn't cold. Nothing was like it is in the movie.

Polly restarts the film, saying, "You've got to have a story. Will

Bugsy succeed or won't he? Will Ginger betray him? Will Meyer save him? Who took all that money and where is it? Is love blind? Will Bugsy wise up in time? He won't, so bang bang, they kill him." She makes a circle on her face like the circle Bobby made. "The end of a dream," she says. "So sad. Sad sad sad. Boo hoo, boo hoo."

The twins aim tiny finger guns at Bobby and say, "Bang bang."

"I'll be back soon," Bobby says.

"Bang bang," the twins say, jabbing at Bobby.

Alice grabs the twins' hands, squeezing their fingers together. She's mad, wants them to stop saying *bang bang*. "No no," she says. The girls, pink-eared and blotchy, cry and pout. They screw their lips tight. They've turned their faces inside out. Alice lets go of their fingers, pats their heads and their cheeks, and their arms, then signs, "Say bye-bye to Grandpa." The twins glare at Alice. "Grandpa's going bye-bye," Alice signs. Polly freezes *Bugsy*.

The twins wobble toward Bobby. They're top-heavy, like they're on the bank of a fast river and could easily fall in. They come in close, sign and say, "Bye-bye," over and over. Bobby offers them his baby-wave, wondering what it is he's tapping out here. What telegram is he sending?

Polly says, "Popcorn," and starts *Bugsy*.

Backing out of the driveway, Bobby sees Lewis hop into a limo in front of the house. Lewis's buddy works for Silver State Limousine and drives Lewis anywhere he wants to go. The tree trimmers left the lawn clean as scrubbed tile.

Bobby takes Tropicana to The Strip where he slows and catches a red light so he can check out Archie Cohen's sign. It's kitty-corner to where he's stopped. Just above the sign's base, the gold letters now say ENTERTAINMENT. Who, he wonders, in this brain-dead town would have noticed? How had pea-brained Archie Cohen caught it?

At the Neon Handmaid, Bobby orders a beer. The topless dancers two-step and boot-scoot to music that is some kind of bastard mix of jazz and country. Their boob jobs are sad. Their dismay, thick. The women have an ounce or two of sway left in their bodies, like the loser of a five-set tennis match waiting for the last serve, full of hope, but it's clear that it's forty-love, that it's game, set, and match. Bobby sips his beer. He hates the schoolteachers and bankers dressed like cowboys in here. And their drinks. A Colorado Bulldog. Something called Between the Sheets. Outside, in the parking lot, those are Volvos and BMWs angled like a crossword puzzle so as to avoid getting their doors dinged.

Bugsy Siegel killed people. He was a triggerman, a torpedo. He carried a gat. They say he'd kill you for fifty bucks and the jump-start it gave him. This amazes Bobby Book. Bugsy Siegel rubbed people out. Think about it. Benjamin "Don't Call Me Bugsy" Siegel. The Bug. Bugs.

Bobby wants to put a stop to people calling him "Best Buy." BB, he doesn't mind.

He wonders if any of these sad sacks in this bar are doing what he's doing? On Mondays he buys eight pairs of brand-new Jockey briefs. He wears fresh ones every day, then tosses them in the trash. He can't tell you why. Has no reason he could put into words. Polly has noticed, he's sure, but she's not said anything. The bastard jazz and country moans, and Bobby sits over a second beer and runs through the deaf alphabet, right-handed, then left-handed, a kid taking a pop quiz. He lays his watch next to his coaster that says BEND A LITTLE and times himself. He can buzz through the alphabet in twenty-five seconds right-handed, thirty seconds left-handed.

Bobby's involved with a deaf woman, and he worries over the psychology of that. What's the taboo here? Does he want to get into his own daughter's pants? If he read more, he thinks, he'd know why. If he'd paid attention in school, done his homework. If he'd studied more than market analysis in college. Deaf daughter, deaf girlfriend. Both with red hair. What would a shrink say? Does God have an opinion? In Genesis? or Job? in the New Testament? Thou shalt not . . . what?

Her name is June, and her hair has the heft and presence of a candelabrum. It's that color the bottom of copper pans can be, and she's one inch, as she puts it, from being thirty. Time and again she looks at Bobby the way the twins do. She silently hikes around in his brain. He knows she's saying, *What does he want with me?*

Her world.

He wants her world.

When June talks, when her hands cut and paste, the world is cinematic. It's dance and music, and he walks into it. He's been invited to the party. Her hands are smart. They're hands he imagines a potter would have. Bobby's wanting June is not because of Alice. Alice is not part of this picture. Fuck the psychoanalysis.

Bobby finishes his beer, calls in a pizza, and drives out to June's apartment on Spring Mountain Road. A block away, he picks up the pizza. His tape deck is playing Jim Croce, who's singing, "Sometimes, they say, you eat the bear / Sometimes the bear eats you." Genuine saxophone. Croce and a cartoon tenor sax on rummy legs and the mop and the brooms and the water pails from *Fantasia*—it's a big-time Technicolor Hollywood dance number in Bobby's head, the sax wailing, the mop and the brooms and the pails bebopping, Croce whining, "OuOuOuOuee / For the rest is just a tragic tale. / Wasn't worth it. Wasn't worth it. Because five short minutes of love / done brought me twenty long years in jail."

June gave Bobby a key to her apartment, but he always knocks twice, then rings. Her dog answers, barks three times, smacks the door, then runs to June. The dog's name is Shaker, because, June says, he's a plain and simple dog.

So this evening Bobby knocks, and Shaker barks and whacks the door. In a couple of minutes June opens it, and Bobby shows her the pizza. The box is hot and hard to balance on one hand, but he's got a gift in the other one. Her face goes *ugggh*, and she grabs her stomach. "I'm having a fat day," she signs. She takes the pizza, and he follows her toward the alcove that is her kitchen. He lays her gift on a coffee table.

"For me?" she signs. June's gotten Bobby a plate. He finds a knife, shows it to her, points at the pizza, and says, "Sure?" She holds her belly. Bobby, showing her the knife, says, "What did the knife say to the other knife?"

"Looking mighty sharp today," she signs.

"You've heard it."

"One of Margot's favorites." Margot is her niece.

Bobby had tried to call June "Sugar" one night and couldn't figure out how to sign it, how he could make it a name. He wrote on a piece of paper, "How do I call you *Sugar*?"

She didn't sign her answer. She wrote under his note, "You don't. Ever." She folded the slip of paper into a square, put it in his wallet, and signed, "Read that when you're feeling stupid."

They carry the pizza into the living room, and June picks up her gift. It's Bobby's first to her. She holds it in her lap and signs, "A funny shape."

He makes a tearing motion, says, "Open it."

She rips the wrapping paper off. Bobby says, "It's a boomerang," and makes a throwing motion. He's thinking, How do you sign *boomerang*? June's gripping it like she's going to try it out. Bobby signs, "Let's go across the street." There's a golf course on the other side of Spring Mountain Road. He says, "We'll toss it like pros. I can show you."

She signs, "When pigs fly," and hands the boomerang to Bobby. She signs, "Sweetheart," her hands, in fists, together, knuckle to knuckle, their backs to Bobby, her thumbs up and wiggling. *Heads nodding to each other.* She doesn't finish what she's saying. Leaves it at Sweetheart.

He says, "What?"

She signs, "Let's make love."

They do, right here in the living room, on the couch, one leg up, one on the floor. Afterward, they lie in the dark and don't talk. The only light in the room comes from an outside lamppost. Someone is swimming in the pool that sits in the middle of the apartment complex. Whoever it is dives in, swims one lap, hops out, and then dives back in. It's so quiet Bobby hears footsteps as the person pads back to the diving board. On the floor, beside his pants and shirt, are his brand-new briefs. They glow in the dark. They're as bright as sunlight on a windshield. Curled up by the side of the couch is Shaker.

There was a time, Bobby has read, when the church believed you couldn't go to heaven if you couldn't hear. You were outcast. God didn't want you.

Bobby signs to Shaker, "How ignorant do you think I am?"

The dog says, "As much as me."

Only then can Bobby sleep.

He wakes when June touches his shoulder. She pillows her cheek in the palm of her hand, asking, *Sleep?* Or is she asking, *Home?* Does he need to go home? She signs, "Sleepy." He's not sure if she's telling him that she is sleepy or asking if he is. He says, "I've got to get going."

Bobby comes into the house through the garage and can hear Alice and the twins leaving by the front door. They've stayed late, past eleven. He hurries in to say goodbye, and the twins run to him. They're cranky. Bobby knows he smells like June, and he is ashamed. He crouches and hugs the twins. He says, "How old are you?"

They say, "Five," and hold up three fingers.

He says, "How cute are you?"

They say, "Very cute."

Alice leans over and signs to them, "Kiss the baby," and the twins hug and kiss each other. They stick together like gum.

Bobby says to Polly, "How was the movie?"

"It was okay," she says. "They haven't changed it since we saw it. Same ending. Very sad and, as you pointed out, not true."

Alice has read their lips. She signs, "Warren Beatty is a hunk."

Polly says to her, "Go home to your husband and pretend."

Bobby helps Polly clean up the family room. Popcorn's scattered like confetti on the floor and couch. Polly and Alice drank a six-pack of Coke, and the twins have left wads of bread on a plate and smashed into the coffee table. No one rewound the video, so Bobby does that. One balloon teddy bear has been popped, but the other one sits on the floor watching the dead television.

Polly is already in bed when Bobby comes in and sits by her legs. He's changed his shorts, has tossed the ones he wore in a garbage can out back. The light is off, but he can see her face. He signs, "Sugar."

"Bugsy Siegel," she says.

"No," Bobby says, "William Powell, *The Thin Man*. That's what he called Mrs. Charles. He called her Mrs. Charles, or he called her Sugar."

"Pretty old-fashioned," she says.

Bobby says, "I'm just an old-fashioned guy, Doll."

"We'll see."

"Bugsy's Virginia died in Salzburg," Bobby says. "Maybe suicide. Maybe they rubbed her out." He stands up and does a few jumping jacks, breathing hard, talking, saying, "Bugsy liked calisthenics. Every morning, one two three four." Bobby sits on the bed and catches his breath. Then he signs, "I will always love you." *I*—he points at himself. *Love*—he holds his hands on top of each other over his heart. *You*—he points at Polly. *In the future*—his flat hand moves up and away from his right temple. *I*—he points to himself again. *I love you in the future I.*

Bobby's brewing coffee when his father comes in the next morning, carrying with him the outlaw smell of cigars and beer. He's slung his jacket over his shoulder. His silk shirt looks bloodless.

"Tell me you won big," Bobby says.

Lewis pulls out the pockets of his baggy pants and lets them sag on his thighs.

"They wiped you out?"

"You're looking at a big loser."

Bobby pours Lewis a cup of coffee, says, "Tell me why Bugsy Siegel put a gun in your ear."

"He was a bug," Lewis says. He waves the coffee off and smacks his forehead to show just how dumb Bugsy Siegel was, then tugs at his crotch to show what Siegel thought with. "All that shit about visions in the desert was just that—shit. Bugsy Siegel was full of it."

Outside the tree trimmers have begun work. The kid shimmies up a tree, grabs a limb, and twirls himself into the foliage. The old guy sets up their sign near the curb. He steps back, sizes it up. CAUTION, it says. MEN IN TREES. What, BB wonders, does the old guy think? The kid appears, disappears, reappears slippery as a squirrel. On the lawn, a plastic case lies open. The old guy takes out a torch, lights it, and starts burning weeds in the gutter.

By nine, Bobby's standing in the dirt looking up at Archie Cohen's sign. Archie's wearing light green today and a black tie. He had called at eight, said, "We need to look at the sign."

"It's fixed," Bobby said. "I saw it."

Archie said, "Humor me."

So Bobby has humored him.

Archie's complaint is that the color around the E in ENTERTAINMENT is darker than the original background color. "They can't match the color?" he says.

Bobby says, "It has to fade. If they paint it to match, it'll look bad in a couple of weeks."

"It looks like a patch," Archie says. He taps his fortune-cookie nose.

Bobby turns on him, gets so that he's face to face with Archie Cohen. Could he, he'd jam a hook up Archie Cohen's nostril, snag the Chinese fortune, and unfurl it like bunting as he pulls it out. Archie runs his hand up and down inside the lapels of his light green suit. He straightens his tie. Bobby points at Archie's chest. He is signing, *You*. Right now Bobby couldn't talk if God asked him to. He makes the sign for *three*, resting his thumb against his own nose. Then he bends slightly his two extended fingers and wiggles them. *Insect*. He is signing, *You are a bug*. His hand flicks through the alphabet, spells out Archie Cohen. *You are a bug, Archie Cohen*.

Archie stumbles backward toward his Jaguar.

Bobby spells out his message. His hand scuttles through the letters. "Y-o-u a-r-e a b-u-g, A-r-c-h-i-e C-o-h-e-n." His hand hiccups, it's so fast.

Archie has climbed into his car and is rolling backward when Bobby slaps his bird finger against the driver's side window. That middle finger, Archie Cohen can understand that. Bobby's ring hits the glass hard as a rock. Dust is rising behind them. Bobby's left hand is signing, is saying, "What are you going to do, Archie Cohen? Are you going to plug me, Archie Cohen? Are you carrying, Archie Cohen? You going to rub me out?"

Cohen flips a U, floors it. He bounces onto Tropicana and is gone.

Bobby starts climbing one of the steel girders that support Archie Cohen's sign. He's seen the construction workers do this when they're in a hurry, when they've forgotten a tool and don't want to undo their ladders, when they've left a wrench on the deck and need to fetch it. Fifteen feet up the girder there are steel bars welded to it. You just have to reach fifteen feet. Then you've got a ladder to use. Problem is, Bobby climbs like a tadpole, and he's stuck twelve feet up, has breaststroked his way this far, and now he can't move. He's a granny knot tied to the beam. There's a scientific explanation for this. Fat cells? Glycogen? Bobby "Best Buy" Book has used up his glucose or whatever it is that gives energy to his muscles, and now he's holding on for his life. Can't go up, can't slide down. He wanted to scramble onto the painters' deck and sign something big, something in capital letters. He was thinking he could twist his body into alphabet. He'd stand tall for the I. He'd flip himself around like Lewis and contort himself into an N, then spread his arms for a T. He'd get everyone's attention. He'd be like one of those radio guys who are always living on some sign for some idiotic reason. They lost a bet on the Super Bowl, something like that. But Bobby's not moving an inch. He's hanging on to this girder for his life. Here he is, the INtertainment—I-N-T-E-R-T-A-I-N-M-E-N-T. Bobby "BB" Book, he's the guy who put the I back in entertainment. If he could get up there, that's what he'd sign. INtertainment. I-N-T-E-R-T-A-I-N-M-E-N-T. Over and over and over again.

But he's glued to this girder, and all he can think about is what he thought about when he was a kid. Suppose you're in an elevator and you're going up. You're not very far up, maybe three floors, maybe five, and the elevator slips. It starts to fall. The safety brakes fail. The elevator's picking up speed and you're going to be crushed. If, just as it hit, at that instant, you could time it, if you could jump in the air at the exact second the elevator hit, would you survive? Would you be treated at the scene for minor injuries and sent home to rest?

LATE-NIGHT TV

There are two houses behind where me and my wife Kay live. We're on the frontage road, quarter of a mile across an open field from the freeway. You take a dirt road south of us to get to the houses. There used to be just one brick two-story and a sheep camp back there, both lost under a clump of Chinese elms. Then last summer flatbeds hauled in a shabby, birthday-cake pink clapboard and wedged it between us. Coming in, they wiped out a maple Kay had just planted. The clapboard is now aluminum siding, and it looks good, but you've got to wonder about what's underneath all that smoothness. It was ragged and tilted bumping along the dirt road. The roof's still bad. A picture window on the west side faces us, and the husband—Mr. Aluminum Siding, Kay calls the guy—sits in a wingbacked chair all day and stares into the room he's in. His venetian blinds yanked up, you can see him from our kitchen. He's always wearing a base-ball cap.

Twice, maybe three times a week, a pizza delivery boy slams to a stop in our driveway and lopes like keep-on-truckin' up the front steps. "You want the second house around to the side," we tell him. "That's not for us," we say. "You want Cook's." It's always a different kid. They must come and go like hotcakes. Sometimes it's a girl, her hair bunched up and frayed under her blue cap with its red bill. "There's a dirt road south of us," we tell them. I even point. Kay, she shuts the door and lets them deal with it. For some reason, the kid always gives the house number above our door the evil eye, as if I'd lie to him. What does he think, that we're setting him up, that he'll ease his truck along the dirt road, high-center it in a rut, and then get jumped and die defending his pizzas? You can't blame them, though—can you?—given what we see on the TV night after night. All those real-life cop shows. Every day it's your money or your life.

I say to each new pizza kid, "The road's right there, on the other side of the lilacs." Sometimes, even if I'm in my socks, I'll step onto the porch and show the kid where to turn because you can't see the road from here. I'll say, "Don't go to the first house, the one with the siding. You want the brick one in the trees." They don't seem to get it. What's so tough? You back out our driveway, turn your steering wheel so you're facing south, drive a hundred feet or so, and make a left, looking for brick, not siding. I mean they go on and deliver the pizza, but they slouch down the steps like this is some kind of trick I'm playing on them, like, just for a joke, I tied their shoes together and gave them a hotfoot at the same time.

One time Kay went ahead and paid for the pizza, and sitting on the wood patio I built this summer, we ate most of it. We could see Mr. Aluminum Siding in his window, and we could see a corner of Cook's place. Kay tore off bite-sized pieces and tossed them to Hoop, our dog. We had two twelve-inchers on our hands, both plain cheese, food called in by people of limited imagination.

We'd have ordered Canadian bacon, pineapple, black olives, green onions, and pepperoni. Kay sliced up some olives and onions and sprinkled them on. My belief is pizza ought to be a pig-out, trough time, down-on-your-knees, face-in-the-food, no knives or forks allowed.

Getting into the second box, I said to Kay, "Let's not look a gift horse in the mouth," and, slipping Hoop a piece, she said, "Or turn down manna from heaven."

I said, "Or toss the baby out with the bathwater."

"We must give thanks when thanks is due," she said.

"Many thanks."

"Thank you kindly."

"A bunch."

"A heap."

We raised our Cokes toward Cook's and said, "God bless you."

Just as the insects arrived for the evening, we dragged ourselves inside. A pizza truck was working its way along the dirt road. Sex that night was onion breath and heavenly, and about 2 A.M., sitting at our kitchen table, I polished off the last gluey wedges of pizza, thinking, *Just the ticket.*

This morning early, Hoop barks to go out, and I climb out of bed, and I'm doing my penguin walk through our kitchen, thinking how someday the baby Kay and I are having—our first, a girl— will feel her own age like knots in her joints and braids in her bones and walk the way I'm walking. Then I stop, because outside, the trees, the lawn, the fence, the mountains, the valley, everything is saffron. It's late fall, but I've never seen a daybreak like this. TV news has been reporting sunsets the color of copper pots and some connection to a volcano that erupted a year ago. This, however, on the other hand, is sunrise. TV says the air is full of sulfur. Some big-time photographer is flying from continent to continent taking pictures of the sunsets. I'd like to snap one of what I'm seeing right now. It's like I'm standing here inside a stained glass window.

Hoop barks and whacks at the back door, and I open it, then the screen. Mr. Aluminum Siding is in his chair. It's about quarter to seven. A cop is parked in front of Cook's. His cruiser's door is open, and I can hear calls coming in. There's no one in sight. The engine's running, and it's cold enough that the exhaust is puffy and blue. The only other noise is the morning commute on the freeway. Traffic sounds like the wash of ocean you hear when you listen to a seashell. Up on Cook's lawn is an ambulance. All this happened, and I didn't hear any of it.

Mr. Aluminum Siding, he's watching TV, I guess. Too early for that, to my way of thinking. This world, its comings and goings, it's all none of his business.

Kids on bicycles pedal up the dirt road and skid to a stop. One, wiggling his front tire, is trying to keep from putting his feet on the ground, but has to give it up. All of them are wearing black high-tops. Looks like they've stuck licorice on their feet. They've twisted their caps around backward and wear shirts and shorts so big it's like they're in a gunnysack race.

Hoop rushes the fence and barks. A kid barks at him. One growls. Hoop, on the grass, zipping along the fence, is white and flashy, is as quick and jerky as one of those spots of sun that leap off the crystal face of your wristwatch and bounce around the walls of whatever room it is you're sitting in.

I say, "Knock it off." I'm yelling at Hoop, but want the kids to know I'm here.

The cop comes around the ambulance and stares over the way cops do, like they can see through all the world's crap including yours. He's cop fat—you know what I mean? Got one of those rhino bodies. There is, as Kay always says, thunder in that kind of thigh. Hoop keeps barking, so I say, "Hoop." The cop ducks into the front seat of his cruiser.

"Hoop," a kid yells. He's making circles on his bike in the dirt, and Hoop is digging to get at him. They all yell. "Hoop. Hoop. Hoop."

Hoop won't come in, so I go out, have to pick him up and carry him. We stand just inside the screen door, and Kay passes behind us. We had it confirmed yesterday that she's expecting a girl. Our baby's heart has formed and begun to beat. Pip pip pip, it says. Imagine her heart, small as a peanut. It's making red blood cells like mad. Kay's started vitamin B for muscle tone and E for oxygen. I've quit cigarettes. We're both thirty-five, graduated from high school together all those years ago, then attended the local college, and this girl is our first, as I said. We waited until I got into management at ShopKo, got our future in order, bought this house, and we've gone into this with our chins firm and our guard up.

I say to Kay, "I bet Cook died."

"No," she says. She puts her hands on my shoulders. "I hope not."

I say, "There's a cop and an ambulance, and no one seems to be in a hurry."

Kay looks out the screen's storm window and says, "God bless him if he did." She crosses the hallway into the bathroom.

We don't really know Cook, just the name. At some point, usually after I've said to the pizza delivery kid, "That's not for us, that's for Cook," the kid'll say, "You're not Cook?" Their brain clogs up. It's tilt time in their head.

Cook's got a wife. Most days about noon, a Dodge the color of brownies, squared off and as big as a barge—one of those cars you know they no longer make parts for—dips and sways stiff as plywood down the dirt road and stops short of the frontage road where a woman sends a kid to check their mailbox. The kid could easily get hit. People fly along this street, and the boxes sit up against it. The Cooks might have three kids or a dozen. It's hard to know. They all look like they're about eight or nine. Children look alike to me, and theirs seem rough and slow, like they're torn at the edges and the seams, like Mrs. Cook ran out of building blocks early on.

They've also got cats, and Cook boots them around. Near dark, under the Chinese elms, he sits sidesaddle in that brown car or on the tailgate of his truck, legs dangling, and he flips matches at kittens. His kids hop up and down like it's a party. Cook lets the cats breed in their sheds, then sends the boys out to drown the babies or dump them in the fields. We've got two that must be his. One day, out for a walk, trying for that sun-on-your-face feeling, Kay and me, we found an orange one in the high dry weeds. Another cat, long-haired and trowel-faced, walked up on our porch, asking for help. I worry about our baby's being allergic to them. That happens a lot. I worry that we, like Cook, will have to get rid of the cats. Like Cook, but we'll find homes for them. Cook's a tall bent man whose thick jaw slopes like a landslide. He could be forty or sixty. I couldn't tell you for sure.

The cop steps away from his car and heads for Cook's. He tells the kids to take off. One says, "We live here," then catches up to the others, who are letting their bikes carry them down the dirt road. Kay stops behind me, rests her head between my shoulder blades, and says, "It's too early to be awake and on your feet."

"You're sleeping for two," I say. I'm a thirty-five-year-old father-to-be, and—I admit it—I'm a sap.

Mr. Aluminum Siding's wife drives down the dirt road. He hasn't budged.

I go to the bathroom, and when I come back out, the world's lost its saffron color and the ambulance and the cop are gone, noiselessly, like none of this happened, like those aliens and their crop formations. You've seen what they're doing, haven't you? on late-night TV? The experts explain that they're trying to greet us. The wheat crushed into circles, that's their alphabet. One smart aleck said, "They're faxing the world." The Indians, they say the earth is crying in shame.

Did I see a cop and an ambulance?

I'd bet on it.

Mr. Aluminum Siding, he never even glanced over.

Hoop's curled up in my spot on the bed. He peeks at me and I glare back and pat him on the butt, so he scoots over and stretches out between me and Kay.

Two days later a Cook shows up in the obituaries. A young Cook, though. Kay reads the notice to me. The address is right. The picture is of a ten-year-old boy. The write-up says *he returned to his father in heaven after a brave and courageous struggle here on earth.* So, after dinner, when I'm out on the lawn shifting hoses and sprinklers around, trying to water some dry spots before winter hits, and I see Cook walking up the dirt road, I say, "Did you have some trouble the other morning?"

He's slipped the county newspaper from its rubber band and is flapping sections open. We're close enough I could take one giant step and touch Cook. I could knock his cap off. He says, "Trouble?"

"A couple of mornings ago," I say. "I thought I saw an ambulance." I'm trying to unstick the spout on a jammed-up Rainbird, and it's squirting water on my dress shoes.

"Boy's tammy," Cook says, and he pats his stomach.

"Your boy's tummy?"

He nods, tucks the newspaper under his arm, and starts up the road. He tosses the rubber band in our lilac bushes.

I say, "Is he okay?"

Cook stops, says, "Boy's dead."

"Your boy died?"

"Dead as can be," Cook says, and he disappears behind the lilacs.

Inside, Kay is working on her enunciation when I tell her about Cook's boy dying of something to do with his *tammy*. What Kay does is she flattens out her fingers and makes the top of her hand into a ledge and slides it under her chin clear up against her throat so that it tilts her head back a notch or two. Makes her look proud, like that motto for the U.S., like Don't Tread on Me. Her hand under her chin, she runs through her i-n-gs. She says, "Fish-*ing*. Danc-*ing*. Eat-*ing*. Bicycl-*ing*. Be-*ing*." She makes up songs full of *ings*. "I go fishing in the morning," she sings, hand in place, chin up. "I go dashing and skating in the evening." Bluesy stuff. Kay's told me I screw up when I say *human being*. I say, *U-man Bean*, like I'm talking about food. She tells me to work on my *h*'s and my *ings*.

"Cook says *tammy*," I say. Kay elevates her chin and says, "De-liver-*ing*."

The books tell us our baby has a tongue and gums, and teeth are forming. The baby's fussing all day long is her saying she's all ears.

Behind Kay, behind the blinds, is one of those copper sunsets that photographer is looking for. I open the blinds and see Cook drive by. His truck's so noisy it's like a threat. Every time I see it, hear it, I think about those sci-fi films that show us our future, the ones you see late at night on TNT, the ones full of desert and blowing sand and a sun that does nothing but scorch the earth. There are roaming tribes of people who don't wear anything but rags and who were once decent to each other. They drive vehicles held together by luck and need. Everything so bleak you get heartsick.

Through the blinds I see there are thick clouds up against the roof of the sky and there are the mountains below and there is this break between them that is filled with red the color of taillights.

Another saffron dawn, and I'm looking out the small windows over the kitchen sink. Mr. Coffee's on, and I'm melting butter for eggs. It's warm enough that I've latched the windows open. I'm letting the morning soak the room. The only traffic on the freeway is now and then the whine of a semi. Hoop is out back tumbling like a baseball across the lawn. The city has put up flasher barricades where the dirt road meets the frontage road, and a crew is cutting away a strip of pavement. Must have something to do with the sewer. Cook bounces down the dirt road in his phone company truck, a flatbed with a white cab. He works for Mountain West. The truck holds a big roll of cable up near the front. Hard hats and an Igloo water jug sway on an angle-iron rack that runs front to rear along both sides. A yellow ladder, tied to the top of the rack, pokes out over the cab. Above the bumper, at the corners of the flatbed, are Day-Glo orange pylons. They look like budding cow horns. Two rifles hang in the back window. Cook stops and honks. One of the workers signals for him to back up and go around. Cook piles out of his truck, picks up a barricade, and throws it toward our lawn. It crashes into the lilacs. Its yellow light is blinking. "Hey," the worker says. He's a big guy wearing a silver hard hat. I can hear him the way you hear a radio playing far away at night. Cook goes for another barricade, and this guy steps between him and it. He says to Cook, "All you got to do is drive around."

You can do that. You circle the Taylor place to the south, make a horseshoe past their chicken coops and dog runs, slide by their garage, and you're on the frontage road.

Cook points at the guy, and the guy says, "This ain't even a road legally." He's got Cook by six inches and fifty pounds.

Cook stumps around, then kicks the barricade he tossed aside. Then he's after something in his truck and right back out and is strapping on those spikes telephone repairmen use to get them up poles. A long piece of steel runs like a cutlass along the inside of his calf and boot and at the bottom curls outward into a sharp point. It fastens to his leg by two leather straps, one high up around Cook's knee and one low around his boot at the ankle. He faces the big guy and gestures for him to come on. He holds his hands low to the side and flicks his fingers. "Let's see what kind of a man you are," he says.

"You're nuts," the big guy says.

Cook says, "You bet."

The big guy raises his arms and says, "Let's just calm down. Nothing happening here we can't talk about."

"I'm calm," Cook says. "I'm the calmest man on the planet, and I'm a handful."

"You are that."

"Just you and me. Come on."

The big guy walks away.

Cook shoves over a barricade. "Want a piece of me?" he says to the other workers. He smashes the barricade's blinking light, grinds it to pieces under his boot heel, then climbs into his truck, his spikes still on, and rams the barricades. On the frontage road, headed south, he stops, cutting off the street. He jumps out of the truck, grabs a rifle, twirls its butt up against his shoulder, and aims at the workers, who, like cartoon mice, dive into ditches and scramble for cover. Cook is laughing his head off.

All day at work, what I see in my head is Cook sighting down his rifle, then almost going to his knees in the street because he thinks what he's done is so funny. I didn't tell Kay about it when she got up. The baby'd hear. She is, as I said, all ears. About midnight, Kay's asleep, and on late-night TV there's a story about a couple who starved their son to death. They show pictures of the kid, but first the progam's host warns us that what we're about to see is graphic footage. Viewer discretion is advised. In the pictures the boy looks like a tadpole. In one he is smiling like any other kid. In most of them he's bruised or burned, has bumps the size of rats. He's lost teeth and his hair is patchy.

Next day, all day, the way it was with me seeing Cook and his rifle and him almost on his knees in the street, I can't forget the pictures of the boy. I get home, and Kay and I walk Hoop in the park. Kay makes one loop with us, then sits at a redwood bench in a picnic area. Friends told her to go barefoot when she can, so she's done that for the walk. Our Indian summer seems endless. Kay's upset about her hair. It won't behave and has gotten thick as grass and knotty, and it's dry. I hinted I might light up just one cigarette out here in the open, and she said, "Not near me. I'll go up like dry brush." She covered her hair with her hands. The birthmark on her forearm has darkened into a smudge.

Hoop, he's nothing but a high-wire act and muscle dashing back and forth between me and where Kay's sitting. I smile at him and wonder how you starve a child to death. The rest of the family stood by and watched. His brothers and sisters, they even helped the father handcuff the boy to table legs and pipes, and they all ate in front of him. It was his punishment. I'm not making any kind of one-to-one connection, I'm not saying Cook is doing anything like that, but after Kay and Hoop and I get home I walk around to Cook's. The house that stands between us and Cook is shut up like a box. A paper pumpkin's stuck to the front door, and there's a ghost made out of pillowcases sitting on the steps. The blinds are closed. The patch of corn they grew this summer, its stalks stripped, has bleached in the sun and looks like wax paper cut and folded for a grade-school bulletin board. It rustles in the breeze.

Cook's sheep camp's got a tin roof and is painted forest green along its wooden sides. Two boys on his lawn are passing a BB gun back and forth and shooting at birds. One has black hair. The other one is blond. They're wearing T-shirts that come to their knees and say Utah Jazz on the front. The boys have crew cuts, but their hair is long at the neck and flows like a waterfall between their shoulders. I say, "Is your dad around?"

Now they act like the pizza delivery kids. Dumb as dirt. The black-haired one has a balloon tied to his belt. It floats above his head. It's grape colored and puckered from being old. On it is the white outline of a cat sitting on its haunches and facing straight at me. The balloon says From Your Doctor For Being Good. The words circle the cat.

"Is Mr. Cook your dad?" I say.

They act like I've asked them to multiply five-digit numbers.

A young version of Cook jumps from the back of the sheep camp. Maybe this Cook is twenty. I've never seen him before. He's wearing a plaid workshirt and Levi's. No shoes. His feet are so white you'd think he'd stepped in paint. He points that Cook chin at me and says, "You live up front."

"I'm Oliver," I say.

"Sure," he says. "You got that pretty wife."

The boy with the black hair shoots the BB gun into the trees and says, "Shit."

"Jacob," the man says to him.

"It flew," the boy says. "Didn't hit it."

"No reason to profane," the man says.

I say, "I was wondering if there's anything I could do to help. Mr. Cook said his boy died. Something was wrong with his stomach."

"I'm Mr. Cook," he says.

I say, "So the boy was yours?" This doesn't seem possible. Maybe he's twenty-five, but not thirty, not old enough to have a ten-year-old boy.

"The boy was mine," he says. He takes the BB gun from the kid Jacob, cocks it, aims at a bird, and fires. He says, "Shit. Damn. And son of a bitch."

The boys think this Mr. Cook is funny, and this Mr. Cook, he thinks he's funny himself. He cocks and shoots again. Some leaves, carrying with them the colors of fall, flutter to the ground. This Cook says to me, "What was it you were going to do?" and he hands Jacob the gun. He flicks the balloon with a finger.

Jacob says, "Cut it out."

"Cut it out," Cook says. He throws a punch but pulls it short one inch from the kid's shoulder and says, "You telling me to cut it out?" Jacob points the BB gun at Cook, and Cook slaps it so hard it bangs against the kid's jaw. "Don't," is all Cook says, and he puts a finger as white as his feet in the boy's face.

I step closer and say, "I came to offer a hand."

"You going to bring my boy back to life?" Cook says. "Can you raise my boy from the dead? Can you do that?" He's getting jumpy.

I raise both hands, telling him I meant no harm.

He says, "Dead be dead."

"I'm sorry for you."

He says, "My father did that once."

"Did what?"

"He raised my boy from the dead," Cook says. "He put his hands on my boy's head and resurrected him in the name of the Lord. Right away, my boy, he walked around, he ate, he shot one of these BB guns." Cook takes the BB gun from Jacob and points it at me. He sights down the barrel at my forehead, at my nose, at my chest. Then he lowers the gun and says, "But it didn't stick. He died again, like you said, and there wasn't anything left in him for Mr. Cook to bring back to this world."

I stand still. I'm saying, "I'm listening."

He says, "You box?" He puts his fists up.

Before I step into something smelly here, I turn away and start down the road, headed home.

He says, "Mr. Cook was a boxer. Now he gets headaches. Forty years after the fact, he gets headaches. He wallows like a pig in the bathtub, and we get the water hot as we can. We boil him pink, and he sucks a lemon, and in the morning the headache is gone. He says the blows, they're catching up to him."

I come back toward this young Mr. Cook, who is bent like his father. The blond kid pumps air into the BB gun and aims it directly above my head.

"Clyde," Cook says.

The boy says, "You did."

Cook grabs the boy by the shoulders and says, "I didn't. I never did anything like it."

The boy lets the barrel drag in the dirt.

I say to this Cook, "These boys yours, too?" Both of the boys, they look healthy and mean, eyes like cuts. They look like they were carved out of rock and brought to life under the older Cook's hands.

Young Cook says, "One is. One isn't."

I say, "You Cook's oldest?"

"I am."

I say, "If there's anything I can do, you let me know. Pass along my offer to your father. It's for both of you."

The next time I see Cook he's pulling his garbage can up the dirt road, and he's wearing a gun. You'd expect a six-shooter, but his is like one you see in those real-life cop shows. It's the gun the homicide detective wears under his jacket. Cook keeps it in a black piece-of-pie holster snapped to his cowboy belt, and it sits on his hip, tilted like the heads of those nodding dogs you see in the back windows of cars.

I'm in the kitchen, and Kay's in the living room practicing her *wh*'s. *Wh*-o, *wh*-at, *wh*-en, *wh*-ere, *wh*-y, *wh*-ich. You're supposed to be able to blow out a candle six inches away. Not that Kay uses candles. Her hair's still a fire hazard. I pour her some orange juice, and Hoop follows me in with it. I say, "Cook's carrying a gun," and offer her the juice.

"Canned?" she says.

Hidden sugar. I forgot.

She sips the juice and says, "Stay away from Cook." Kay's cheeks are blotchy. The mask of pregnancy. By her side is a bowl of dry shredded wheat squares she's eating.

I say, "I bet it's the city. I bet the city's after him. They're not going to let him get away with pointing a rifle at people and destroying city property. He's armed himself."

Kay hands me the glass of orange juice. She took two sips.

"They'll shoot Cook," I say.

"Over barricades?"

"He'll push their buttons."

Hand under her chin, Kay tilts her head up and says, "*Wh*-ich witch was it *wh*-o was *wh*-ere she was not supposed to be *wh*-en *wh*-at happened happened and *wh*-y was she *wh*-ere she was *wh*-en it happened?"

I signal for Hoop to follow me, and we dump the juice in the sink, rinse the glass out, and head for the backyard. Behind us, we hear, "And *wh*-y was the witch *wh*-ere witches ought not be?" I open the screen, and Kay says, "Stay away from that guy."

And I do, for two days, but then the pizza delivery kid shows up at our door and I pay for the pizzas. I look at my watch and say to him, "You almost didn't make the thirty minutes."

"That's not us," he says.

"Sure it is." I tap my watch.

"That used to be us," he says. "But not anymore." The kid's as glum as bad weather. Wouldn't know a joke if it whacked him upside the head. "They'd take the money out of our paychecks," he says.

I say, "That's a gyp."

He rubs his face.

I say, "I was a busboy one year. I had to pay when people walked off with things. The spoons, napkins."

He shakes his head like he can sympathize.

The pizzas cost me thirty-seven dollars. I tell the kid to keep the change from two twenties. Kay's deep into a nap, so I lock the doors and head for Cook's. Hoop is in our backyard, and he barks as I cross the lawn to the south. He can see me through the chain-link fence. "It's only me," I say. "Relax." I tell him he's a good boy.

Our maple fills with starlings this time of year, and they're noisy. I pass by the tree and they fall silent, but don't fly off. It's like I've tossed a cloak over them.

There's a white swing set and a wading pool in the front yard of the house between us and Cook's. The swing set has a slide attached to it. A wheelbarrow at one end is tipped upside down. You climb on it to get to the slide steps. The pool has about an inch of rust-colored water in the bottom. The Halloween decorations are still up. I never see these people outside. I haven't seen Mr. Aluminum Siding for days. They must have kids, but I've never seen any. Right now, it's as if they've sealed up the house, as if they've been murdered and left to rot. Some nights, though, I'm up late and I hear big-band music coming from their place.

Older Cook answers his door, and I hold up the pizza. "Delivery," I say.

He edges his screen open.

"Is this Cook's?" I say.

Cook steps out.

"It's a joke," I say. "You know me. I'm from the house up on the frontage road."

He's wearing his pistol.

"Three family-sized, plain pizzas," I say.

He says, "What is this?"

I tell him the delivery boy came to our place by mistake and explain that I wanted to help if I could so I paid for the pizza. "Did your boy tell you I came by the other day?" I say.

Cook won't take the pizzas. Young Cook is walking over. He's shoeless again.

I say, "I wanted to help with your loss."

"Our loss?"

"With your grief."

"Ain't no grief here."

Cook's son says, "This is the guy who knows how to box." He throws uppercuts.

"That right?" Cook says. "You know how to box?"

Screw this. I set the pizza on his porch and am headed out of here.

"You know how to throw a punch?" Cook says. His son is jabbing at a tree trunk. "Straight out," Cook says. "Don't wind up with a roundhouse haymaker like they do on TV. Keep your elbows in."

I've reached the edge of his lawn when he says to his boy, "Pay the man for the pizzas." I keep walking, and there's a shot behind me. The starlings burst as loud as a car wreck from our maple tree. Hoop barks. Cook's come down his porch, and he's pointing his gun at me, at my heart. He says, "My boy here is going to pay you for the pizza."

I say, "I don't want to be paid."

Cook aims at my feet and walks toward me. He says, "You want to be social, is that it?"

"I was just thinking about your boy."

"You came all the way around here up that dirt road just to be friendly," he says. "You want to be neighborly." His son is walking in small circles, wired, like a hen in a coop. "Be social, then," Cook says. "Dance." His son's at my shoulder, and Cook's still pointing his gun at my feet. "Come on, neighbor," Cook says. "Dance. It'll make you feel real good. I'm just trying to help you." He grabs his nuts, says, "Right here. You'll feel all zingy right here." He jerks at his crotch.

I could heave, could vomit.

Cook holsters the gun, and his son hands me forty dollars. Older Cook says, "That cover it?"

I take the money.

He says, "The gratuity?"

I tell him I tipped the boy.

"Not the boy," Cook says. "You."

Of course, I think. How stupid of me.

His gun's out again, and he waves it at his son, saying, "Tip the man, Vaughn." Vaughn hands me a five. I study Cook, then his son, and then I fold the bill and stuff it in Cook's son's shirt pocket, and I walk down the dirt road, step into one of those sunsets that a photographer would kill for. You can smell the sulfur in the air. The picture I'm seeing of the west mountains and the sky, that picture starts to drip saffron until I'm covered in it.

Kay's on our lawn, near a sprinkler. She heard the shot, I suppose, and she is standing here anchored in that pose women strike when they're nine months along rather than the three months Kay is. She's backlit by the sunset, elbows out, hands on her lower back, as if she's going to have the baby this minute.

But it's the future I'm seeing here. It's not now. I'm seeing us years from today. What a world it is. Our girl—we're calling her Brittany—she's about three and is standing beside Kay. Behind Brittany is our son Mark, her twin. The sonogram, it turned out, lied. Mark was there all the time, hiding behind our girl, probably making rabbit ears behind her head, which is what he's doing right this minute here in the future, turning everything— this saffron day, the pizza, Cook, Cook's boy, his gun—into a bad thought. Kay, in this future I'm seeing, is carrying our third child. We're almost forty, and this one will be our last. We planned this.

We're alive in this stained glass window. Hoop is barking and digging. He wants to save us all.

Years from today—you can imagine it, can't you?—in a few minutes, we'll be inside, celebrating the twins' birthday. We'll blow out candles. Who, we'll sing, and why and when and where and what.

Up the dirt road comes a red Thunderbird I've only seen once or twice. It's lifting dust into the saffron day. The garage door on the house between us and Cook starts to open, and the woman driving the Thunderbird whips into the driveway. The man in the passenger's seat is handsome. He's wearing aviator glasses and a baseball cap. Behind me, Cook's screen whacks shut. Five boys are running toward Cook's.

Inside the garage the woman climbs from the car, reaches through the front seat, and takes the cap off the man. She puts it on herself backward. She grabs the man by his thick head of hair, pulls him through the car, and lugs him out. It's Safe-T-Man. I know him. He's filled with polyfiber and has latex hands. You can buy him off late-night TV. Safe-T-Man costs $119.95, and a Safe-T-Man Tote Bag is $34.95. He's 5′10″, but looks six foot because he's designed with an extra long torso. Clothing is not included. He weighs four pounds. That's all.

The woman slings him over her arm like a garment bag, and when she turns around she sees me.

To the west, the sun irises out.

Kay—I can hear her. We're go-*ing* go-*ing* go-*ing* around in circles, she is saying. Chin up, she says.

Safe-T-Man.

What a thought.

I mean, correct me if I'm wrong.

PLEASE TO FORGIVE SLOPPINESS

Harry's Uncle Stuck, he lands on Harry and Lyla time and again like something shook from a tree. Life's been, for Stuck, a high-wire act that's left him upside down in untidy corners, feeling lopsided, baleful, his eyes dry and sore, his elbows cut, his nose snotty, and a thumb broken and off-shot for good. It's amounted to the romp and stagger cowboys and cowgirls sing about. Stuck's got bad knees, and his thyroid's been nuked. A month back, he turned fifty-seven.

Tonight he phones Harry and says he's flying in. "Flap flap," he says. "Here I come. U . . . nite . . . ed. Fucking-duck airlines, the red-eye."

"Got a flight number?" Harry says. He's frisking himself and picking up books and setting them down, shuffling through mail and flyers, his hunt for a pen deteriorating into slapstick.

Stuck says, "Yes. Oh, God, yes."

Stuck's phone clanks, then bounces. Goes dead. The line sounds hollow. Harry says, "Stuck?" He's located a leaky ballpoint in the kitchen junk drawer. He blows in the phone. No

Stuck. "You there?" he says. "Stuck?" He covers the mouthpiece, listens, and gets back only the cheap taste and touch of plastic.

"Hello? Hello?" From Stuck's end, more echo than word. "Harry?" Stuck says. It's his footloose voice, the one that tells Harry Stuck's cut and run from some outpost where he's used up his welcome. He's scammed some dupe, left some simple soul holding the bag, and there's something alive and stinky and clawing inside it.

Harry says, "Stuck?"

"Dropped the son-o-bitch," Stuck says.

"What about that flight number?"

"Somewhere. I can't put a hand on it." Dead air, then a rusty phlegmatic cough, followed by that footloose voice. "I can see it with my mind's eye, " Stuck says. "You know what I mean? Clear as mud." He tells Harry how he wrote everything out in script a monk would envy, the time and flight number, on that yellow legal pad. He used a felt-tip Flair.

"Where are you?"

"Oklahoma."

"You're in Oklahoma?"

"Tul . . . sa."

"This tonight is when you're coming? I mean, it's almost tomorrow. Is it tonight or tomorrow night?" Harry wants time and flight. He says, "We're talking about in just a few hours—is that what you're saying?"

"The red-eye. I'm packed. My suitcases are jammed deep into my armpits, and I've got a toe on the threshold. You'll fetch me?"

Harry says, "Count on me."

It means a one-hundred-and-ten-mile, two-hour drive from St. George, Utah, south to Las Vegas, but Harry's done it before.

"My ticket," Stuck says. "It's somewhere. There's stuff all

around. Whose, I don't know. Everything's glued to something else."

Harry says, "You be there. I'll be there."

Uncle Stuck is Harry's blind spot. All Harry's life, Stuck's been Harry's ABCs, his p and his q, his Santa Claus and his Green Hornet all rolled into one.

Jacob, Stuck's older brother who lives in Las Vegas, is wise to Stuck, has him pegged. Holidays, down in Las Vegas, Jacob holds forth on Stuck. "It's not complicated," Jacob says to the odds and ends of the family who've gathered to eat, and he circles the table, a hammerhead shark. "A drunk's a drunk," he says. "It's mathematical, the way shooting pool is mathematics. Ask any drunk you see on any street in any city of the U. S. of A." Then he sits down and dishes up lamb and mashed potatoes. "Drunks kid us," he says, "not other drunks."

Stuck is, plain and simple, a drunk.

Why does Stuck roll cars and walk away slightly battered, pinkie-finger Band-Aids horseshoed over the bridge of his nose, crisscrossing his elbows, but otherwise he's clean as fresh laundry? Why does he rise from the dust like it's Resurrection Day?

Because he's a drunk.

"He's sensitive," the family hums. "Life has hurt him," they sing. All old songs. Unrequited love, a lazy eye at seven, rheumatic fever that scorched his ten-year-old heart.

Jacob's answer?

Simple: "You've heard about God and fools and drunks."

Harry's father, Boyd, who lives two blocks from Harry and Lyla in St. George, the man the family calls The Reverend, not because he's an ordained minister but because he's a morning-noon-and-night preacher of his own word, a gasbag who ought to have a pulpit Velcroed to his chest armpit high—he can tell you about

Stuck. Whatever road you're on The Reverend's been down it, has ridden out its hairpin turns, mapped its dead ends, been bounced around by its potholes, and survived to tell you how to drive it. About Stuck, The Reverend Boyd says, "Stuck's intelligent and his mind has circuits most don't." He grants Stuck inordinate brainpower, a high IQ, a second-to-none vocabulary. "But," The Reverend adds, "he's not smart. Smart is acting right. Smart is studying the road map before you set out. Smart is blankets in the trunk, in plastic, neatly folded, dry and safe, and a first-aid kit and a flashlight and batteries you've checked." The Reverend Boyd says you talk to Stuck the way you talk to a child. "I do," he says. "I point out the trouble around the next bend. I'm his high road. And he listens. I say, 'Stuck, slippery curves ahead.' I say, 'Slow down.'"

Whenever Stuck's around, Stuck tells his own story. It begins and ends, "God got to love me, I'm a failed academic who's come home to roost." The details slip and slide, don't add up from telling to telling, but there are some facts in print if you care to see them. B.A. at UCLA, an M.A. at Stanford. Then three no-shows for Ph.D. orals (talk of hysterical blindness), the last at Berkeley. He fled, sprinted out of Wheeler Hall, hurdled over and zigzagged through the sixties weirdos and hippies, under Sather-gate, along Telegraph, and ended up teaching high school in his hometown, St. George, Utah, until Maureen Bobbs, the algebra teacher, spotted him trying to unlock his classroom, a bottle of rum at his feet, his keys dumped like bad pasta on the cement, one shoeless foot doorknob high, flat against and pushing shut the door he was trying to pull open. There was also a rumor about an undercover cop and an arrest in a gay bar near Nellis Air Force Base in Las Vegas.

United tells Harry that Stuck's plane arrives at 1 A.M., so Harry kisses Lyla so-long and bumps his VW Bug along I-15, a one-man band in the night, driving south through the windy Virgin River Gorge, across a tarp of pitch-black desert to a loopy on-and-off ramp that sucks him into McCarran Airport, Las Vegas, Nevada. A tower spins him up to Parking, and a shuttle whooshes Harry to Stuck's gate. A box-shaped man in a baggy suit tags along, seems to be wherever Harry is, is a swing to Harry as swing set. The man stumps from counter to counter, tickets in his teeth, his bald spot lit up, flashes of neon in his pupils. Soft luggage clings to him, and he's got two-inch cuffs on his pants. He's wearing clogs.

No Stuck.

Harry double-checks the gate number, the flight—where it originated from, which was Tulsa, and when it left. At United Information, a woman punches up names on a computer. Stuck was on board. "Could you have missed him?" she says. "In the crowd?" There's another plane at 7 A.M.

Harry phones Lyla, and she says, "Don't tell me you're surprised."

Harry is, as always.

She says, "What were the odds, Harry?"

"Not good," he says. "But United confirmed it. He was on board."

Lyla says, "Harry." She's right. United's confirmation is meaningless. This is Stuck we're talking about. "Come on home, Harry," she says. "He won't be there at seven either."

The guy in the baggy suit skips by, then back past, then appears around a corner up ahead. The airport's full of sheet metal palm trees, their trunks and fronds defined by green and pink neon. Harry can see The Strip, and except for its glow Las Vegas is as dark as any town at night. He loses twenty at video poker and thirty on the slots. He wishes he drank and wonders what ever happened to real silver dollars. Gambling with tokens is like wearing cloth gloves.

At six-thirty he rents a cart for Stuck's luggage and heads for the gate. The sun pops up, and the flight's on time.

No Stuck.

Harry phones Jacob, who's moved from a split-level brick-and-siding rambler a block from The Strip to a three-story adobe near Red Rock Canyon. Next to Harry is the box-shaped man in his baggy suit. Threads of gold shoot through the guy's jacket. He's shed his luggage and is saying into his phone, "Life is short, Sweetie. Life is short."

Nada—Jacob's word—is what Jacob's heard from Stuck.

Harry says, "You might. I drove down to pick him up and missed him."

"My security doors are locked, dead-bolted and chained," Jacob says. "I've got bars on my windows. I've got Dobermans, and I'll authorize Security to shoot first and ask questions later."

None of this is news.

"Good luck," Harry says.

Jacob says, "I don't need luck. I have weapons."

There's a story about Jacob bringing his family home from Disneyland. Jacob, his wife, their kids, they park in their drive-way, climb out, start unloading. The wife unlocks the front door to the house and runs headlong into Stuck and five—she counts them—wobbly-legged Indians hopping into underwear white as their Hollywood teeth and spilling out of windows. Stuck was the first one over the back fence. There's another story about a Chevy Blazer—Jacob had loaned it to Stuck—left with a flat tire up at Mount Charleston, and there's one about a duplex Jacob owned that burned to the ground.

Harry tries Benny, Stuck's Las Vegas buddy.

Not there. Benny says, "I hear, I'll let you know. You got a number where I can reach you?" Benny is a pit boss at the Horseshoe.

Two nights after Harry returns to St. George from Las Vegas, he and Lyla eat Mexican food up on the Boulevard, and driving back to their place, Harry tuning in the World Series on the radio, they pick up the San Francisco earthquake. Home in their living room, the TV gives them nothing but the disaster. A fire burns in the Marina district, the Bay Bridge has dropped part of itself like a lip, and Highway 880 looks like dominoes. There is something toy-like about the pictures they're seeing.

The Tenderloin district is a mess, and Candlestick Park is falling down.

"I've been there," Lyla says and points at the TV. "I lived in the corner apartment, at the bottom. I stood on that spot. Right there." She taps the screen. She's changed into her robe and has it clamped around her waist. It's eighty outside, but she's cold and has pulled on a pair of Harry's woolly socks. Lyla says, "Give or take a few years, and I could be dead."

The TV replays a shot of a car dropping into the collapsed section of the Bay Bridge. The newspeople don't know if anyone's hurt. "How could anyone not be hurt?" Harry says to the screen. There are no reports of the number of people injured or dead. Harry watches and feels the way he does when he's said something useless or stupid in a crowded room and it's too late to take it back, only right now it's Harry's heart, not his foot, that's a hedgehog in his mouth.

"Do you believe that?" Lyla says. She touches the screen again, and it buzzes. There goes the car, doing what amounts to a headstand off what's left of the Bay Bridge.

Harry settles onto a soft ottoman right in front of the set. Lyla scoots him over, sits, and hunkers up next to Harry.

TV replays the footage of the car. Harry says, "Ka-plunk."
Lyla says, "Look."

Harry is. TV has cut to a long shot of the Marina district. Smoke rises as if there's been mortar fire, hit and miss, but otherwise the houses look snug and safe from this distance. No way would you know that they've fallen in on themselves like a bad cake.

Lyla undoes her hair, saying, "Can you believe this?" She pokes Harry and gawks at the wrecked city. Again, the newspeople run the video of the car skidding, then plunging to the lower ramp of the Bay Bridge. Now an unconfirmed report says a woman was in it and she's dead. Lyla slips off her robe and tosses it toward the couch. It hesitates in the air and falls to the floor. Her T-shirt, all she's wearing, hangs to her knees. TV shows a long shot of the city, and the houses look like candy in a box. "Where's Superman?" Lyla says. "Where the fuck is Superman?"

Harry turns to her.

"You know," she says, "he could reverse things." She raises her pointer finger and twirls it. "You know, fly around the world backward," she says.

There's a tappity-tap-tap of their Alsatian Wolf Dog door knocker, and on his noisy way into the house Stuck says, "Lyla. Harry."

On TV, a helicopter hovers above the Bay Bridge, beating the water into choppy waves. Outside, a car honks, and Stuck opens the screen door and speaks to the disappearing car, talks thickly, mournful as a tiger. He says, "Bye-bye, Baby." Harry's gotten up. A Cadillac U-turns in front of the house and revs through the stop sign on the corner. The driver waves lazily out the window, wigwags *so-long*.

"Jesus," Lyla says. She's glued to the set. A film crew has gotten into the Marina district and is taking live shots. It looks like *Godzilla* footage. Men and women run at the jerky hand-held cameras, end-of-the-world terror in their faces. Sirens wail like prehistoric birds, and water flows like blood and pools in intersections.

Stuck tugs at his Bermudas and tries mightily to rewire his brain. He can't focus on the TV, so he knuckles the doorjamb and says, "Knock on wood."

San Francisco buildings hang tilted on the screen.

Harry and Stuck step onto the porch to collect his luggage, and Harry sees the Cadillac hustling up Main Street past the old college and the Tabernacle. Whoever it is is headed north, not south toward Las Vegas.

Back inside, Lyla hikes up the volume. She's a foot from the TV. The problem for the network reporters is that they can't communicate with their affiliates in San Francisco. The pictures flicker and roll, but the talking comes from anchors who don't know the area. They're two thousand miles away in New York. They've just now been told that what they're showing of Highway 880 is a double-decker freeway. The top lanes collapsed onto the bottom lanes, and it was rush hour when it happened. Lyla says, "Good God." She illustrates the crash, slaps her hands together, palm to palm, one on top of the other one.

"Anyone want M&Ms?" Stuck says, and he lifts a small goldenrod bag from his shirt pocket.

Lyla won't look at him. Harry says, "Maybe later."

"I've come by astral body," Stuck says. He tears a corner from his M&M bag. His luggage has gathered around him like forest animals.

Lyla says, "You're nine sheets to the wind," and she snaps the TV off, collects her robe, and retreats to the bedroom. In there, the portable television comes on, loud, angry. It's Lyla's way of rapping both Harry's and Stuck's knuckles. She's saying she'd like to slap Stuck's face and haul him over hot coals.

"Peanut, not plain," Stuck says and holds out the M&Ms to Harry. "I got a suitcase full. Leftovers from a party that fell through."

Harry holds open his hand and Stuck rolls M&Ms into his palm.

Stuck says, "My craggy brain's on hold." He shrugs his wide-open arms, displays his shabby body, no shoes, cheap Bermudas, a torn Hawaiian shirt the color of pickle relish and mustard mashed together in a tiki bowl, and he says, "Please to forgive sloppiness."

"Sloppiness," Harry says, "I can forgive."

"You missed me," Stuck says. "Not wholly or truly my fault. I had an eye open for you." He shows Harry how, one eye slammed shut, the other one cartoon-big.

The bedroom door slams shut.

It turns out Stuck hasn't been with Benny, but with a woman named Rhonda who lives in Las Vegas. She has about five acres out near The Lakes. Stuck's thinner than is good. Over the past few months, he's sent postcards about his screwy thyroid and drinking radiation malts, but what Harry's seeing is what's left after plague and famine and blockade. Harry's been told Stuck's heart stopped on a golf course and a woman knocked him back into life. The facts are spotty. Bypass surgery is down the road. Right now it's supposed to be diet and walking. No smoking, no drinking.

"You didn't show," Harry says. "At one or at seven."

"I did. The red-eye, there I was."

"What, you sneaked past me?"

"Busy. I was busy. Deep in conversation." Stuck offers Harry M&Ms. Harry shakes him off. Stuck says, "Next thing I know I'm at the Horseshoe. 'Rhonda,' I'm saying to my pal, 'This is Benny. Benny, Rhonda.' Then it's me backstroking in her pool, which is bigger than most city blocks. It's night, stars like diamonds. Ben-

ny's at my side. Pals. Women. Rhonda is a lovely lady. I'm thinking this wouldn't be a bad way to go, to make that final journey."

On the plane, Rhonda had the window seat, and Stuck had the
aisle, no one between them. He passed her her complimentary
drinks, and on a lark she tried on his bifocals, said to Stuck, "I
bet you can see through walls."

To prove he could, Stuck put them on and pointed to the bathroom they were sitting close to. "There's a woman in the john
diddling with herself," he said. "Blonde, top and bottom."

They drank and stared at the door. A blonde came out, saw
them, twisted her skirt, and touched the top button of her blouse,
even blushed.

Rhonda said to Stuck, "You did it."

At her place, there was the pool, a game room, servants, gar-
deners, an eight-foot-high portrait of a husband who was president of the El Cortez, who died one afternoon after lunch. His
secretary said he'd been burping a lot lately. "Come to think of
it," Rhonda said, "he had."

"I looked for you," Stuck says to Harry.

"How hard?"

"Real hard." Stuck fiddles with his M&M bag, then repockets
it. His mind's flagging. He knows where he's to sleep, and Harry
leaves him to it. Lets him carry his own luggage. Harry finds Lyla
sitting on the bed, her feet in his socks, flat and cauldron black
on the carpet. Her earrings, quarter-sized silver disks with road-
runners sprinting across them, dangle and flash in the light from
the TV. "Anything new?" Harry says.

The portable shows Dan Rather stumbling along. What can he
do two thousand miles away? He's vowed he'll be in San Francisco
by morning. The camera zooms in on the Bay Bridge. A helicopter closes fast. Its blades catch sunlight.

Lyla says, "It's like watching TV."

"Bad news usually is," Harry says.

Next morning, Stuck sits on the porch steps reading the *Washington County News*, his orange sweatshirt turned inside out. His sad back lifts and slumps. He knocks ash from his Kool.

Harry stands inside by the big front window in the living room. On the TV, an in-the-field reporter talks about the earthquake, but Harry's turned off the sound. In the kitchen, Lyla and her sister Marge pick at scones and drink coffee. Marge, one year divorced, is here to discuss her new boyfriend, Armstrong Otto. He's a vampire hunter who gave up a cushy job in L.A. and came to St. George because one night about 3 A.M., driving through, he'd seen the undead partying out near the graveyard. His cover is he works as a wrench at the local Harley shop. Harry hears Lyla say to Marge, "We're looking at a real personality disorder here."

"But in all sorts of interesting ways," Marge says.

Outside, Stuck puts aside the newspaper, sets it loosely on a step below him, squirms on his butt, and twists his upper body, a sleepy alligator in mud. His Kool juts cockeyed out of his mouth. He picks up a script he's been studying. Stuck's come to St. George to read at the library with a drama group called the Red Hills Readers. His friend Effie has written a play called *Jack the Ripper and the Daughters of Joy*. Effie's letting Jack's victims get in the last word. The cast is Stuck and eleven women.

Behind Harry, Marge says to Lyla, "Armstrong claims prominent people are involved. St. George big shots. People you and I have eaten with."

"Isn't that always the way it is," Lyla says. "It'll make a great movie."

There's a guy on the TV who's shaved his head and torn the sleeves from the T-shirt he wears. A tattoo throbs on his biceps. He is standing in front of Highway 880. At his back, the freeway has crumbled like cardboard boxes. The man points at the rubble, and a microphone chases his mouth as he turns from side to side. A ladder leans against the concrete retaining wall.

Harry opens the screen door and steps outside. At the breakfast table, Lyla says to Marge, "Really? Wood stakes."

"Aspen," Marge says.

On the porch, Stuck says to Harry, "Cigarette?"

"Had to give them up," Harry says.

"You got to admit it's hard to trust a man who's got no bad habits," Stuck says. "You quit drinking. Now it's smokes. Do you still pull your thing out and make it happy?"

"You're talking about trust?"

"You're killing me."

"That was a hundred miles down and back empty-handed," Harry says. "Not the first time, either."

Stuck flicks his cigarette butt toward the sidewalk and stands up. He's wobbly, shifty as water in a balloon. Each calf has a white elastic bandage around it. Stuck bends over and pulls them up so they support his knees. No socks, just beaded moccasins. His shorts today are stringy cut-off Levi's.

Harry shuffles the newspaper together and drops it inside the front door. He hears Marge say, "That's an old wives' tale. Garlic doesn't work. It only aggravates them. They get angry."

Harry says to Stuck, "There's food inside. Omelets I did myself. I used green peppers and fat-free cheese. The milk is that kind you can see through, and I left the butter off the toast."

"And inside is Marge yakking," Stuck says.

Harry shrugs.

Stuck says, "The boyfriend's really a vampire hunter? This isn't a joke of his?"

"Armstrong's got evidence," Harry says. "He's got proof of the undead in town. He says he's taken photographs and has blood and hair samples. There's something different about their DNA."

"You listened to him?"

"Eavesdropped."

Stuck rolls up Effie's script, taps Harry with it, and says, "How about walking down to Effie's with me?" He lights a Kool, says, "She's got my outfit. I think I'm in top hat and tails."

Harry helps Stuck down the steps. Whatever is wrong with Stuck's knees is crippling. Harry and Stuck poke along the sidewalk, and Stuck hunts for things to sit on every fifty feet, a bus bench, a fire hydrant, fences. Harry leaves him leaning against a retaining wall and hurries into a 7-Eleven to buy Cokes. Stuck wants the biggest they've got.

They pass The Reverend Boyd's. He's under his carport vacuuming his Bronco, wearing a decaying white shirt the color of tartar, a loose black suit slick as shale, and a tie that hangs like a rubber snake from his open collar.

"Hey, Dad," Harry says.

Stuck nods, says, "Reverend."

Reverend Boyd slides in behind the Bronco's open door and goes back to what he's doing. He acts guilty. The man is sneaky-eyed and won't say hello. He peeks at them through the steering wheel. Behind him his carrier pigeons coo in their loft. He disappears under the dashboard, then waddles out of the Bronco backward carrying a box. He lugs it around the side of the house.

"What's up with him?" Stuck says.

"He's hiding something."

"Think he hacked up your mother?"

"It's a possibility."

Two blocks down, they turn a corner and see Effie uprooting the last of her tomato plants that line the irrigation ditch along the south side of her front lawn.

Stuck's cigarette wobbles on his lips. "Horror," he says to Harry. "Effie needs to understand that horror sells tickets." Smoke stings his eyes, and he tears up. His plan for the reading is the curtain rises and you see only the faces of the readers, eleven women and Stuck sitting on stools in a semicircle. Everything else is black. That's how you do the entire play, just the haunted faces talking, a spotlight leapfrogging woman to woman. Stuck, as Jack the Ripper, visible only in candlelight.

Effie's yard is surrounded by a short hedge and oleanders. Her back's to Stuck and Harry. Stuck tosses his cigarette butt into the gutter, rolls the script tight, and shouts through it, "Hey, lady."

You know she knows who it is, but she won't turn around. She's crouched in the garden, collecting stragglers, yanking at plants. A basket of tired tomatoes sits on the lawn.

"Nice ass," Stuck says.

Effie comes up throwing, flings a tomato zipping just to the left of Harry's head before he can blink. "Wrong smart-ass," she says and zeros in on Stuck. He crosses his arms in front of his face, dodges, his knees creaky. Out of the backyard, Effie's dog Poot comes flying, skips like a rock on water. The dog's about as big as a shoe and eats and breaths and defecates in this world like some hybrid thing you'd come upon in the backwoods of Arkansas.

"Go ahead and take your best shot," Stuck says.

"Who?" Effie says. "Me or Poot?" She juggles a tomato hand

to hand and walks over, talking to Harry, saying, "I don't see you enough." The apron she's wearing has lettered across it THE WORST IS YET TO COME. She has this way of walking like she's a troll under a bridge.

"Because you're old," Stuck says.

She says to him, "Because you're not handsome."

"Handsome to you is tall," Stuck says. "If he's tall, he's handsome."

Effie raises her tomato, and Poot adds his constipated bark.

"And redheaded," Stuck says. "You got to be tall and redheaded and handsome for Effie to give you the time of day."

Poot jumps into Stuck's arms, and Stuck pats the dog's head, which is no bigger than a child's fist. He juggles Poot to his hip, and he and Effie hug, abandon themselves to each other. They taught side by side at the high school and have been pals since they were kids. She says, "I need you to stick around and help me. I'll feed you, and we'll take care of a couple of errands. I'll deliver you to the reading."

Stuck lets Poot loose, and the dog gnaws at Effie's sandal. Stuck says to Effie, "I've got one suggestion."

"No suggestions," she says.

Poot sprints for the backyard.

"Just one word," Stuck says.

"No words."

Stuck says, "Horror." You couldn't shut him up if you put a sock in his mouth. He's got hold of a semi and he's going to lift it off the ground. He'll pin Effie's arm behind her if he has to. There's a point to be made. She's got to say uncle. Stuck tells her about the black stage, the spotlight, the candle on an end table under Jack the Ripper's chin. "Spooky," he says. "Don't you think?"

Effie says, "No and no and no."

Stuck has only just begun.

On his way home, Harry sees The Reverend Boyd fiddling with the garbage cans at the side of his house. The Reverend notices Harry and clamps a lid shut.

"Is Mom around?" Harry says.

The Reverend steps through the gate to the backyard and disappears.

At the house, Marge is telling Lyla that the police have been finding pets and small animals dead, their bodies looking as if they've been decompressed, like dried squash in a garden. Only marks on them are two pinpricks on their necks.

"Two kids down fishing the Virgin came upon a pile of dead foxes," Marge said. "Lying under a mesquite bush like empty bags, deflated like beach balls."

Lyla says, "We don't have foxes, do we? This is a desert."

"Larson's daughter found their poodle half-buried under a tumbleweed."

"Harry," Lyla says, "do we have foxes?"

Harry says, "Maybe it was a coyote."

On the TV Dan Rather is interviewing one of the heroes, a man who climbed into the section of Highway 880 that collapsed on itself. The man's hand is bandaged, and he's talking about crushed heads and screams. Dan Rather flew all night to get to San Francisco. The camera cuts to a shot of the freeway. No one knows yet how many people have died. Rescue crews are still reporting moans. The camera catches Dan Rather lowering his mike, ducking his head. The man describes the bodies, the crying, the blood. This guy is making Rather sick.

"You don't have to behead them," Armstrong Otto says. "You see that in the movies. It's part of the lore, but it's not necessary.

What counts is the stake in the heart." Earlier, Marge picked him up at his apartment, and the four of them, Harry, Lyla, Marge, and Armstrong Otto, are going to walk over to the library for the Readers Theater. Right now, they're sitting over drinks. Armstrong opens a brown sack he brought and shows them what's in his holy kit. The sack, from a grocery store, says RECYCLE FOR THE EARTH'S SAKE. The words form a mountain peak. He pulls out a box of salt, incense, a wooden stake, crosses. He wears a gold crucifix around his neck, high up so it shows. He kicked his shoes off when he sat down, and his feet are narrow and curvy like gondolas.

The TV is on, sound mute. Dan Rather has stayed on the job all day. He's worn out, hollow-eyed, his hair fraying.

Armstrong tells them there are rewards for anyone who can bring in a resurrected corpse in what's called the human vampire condition. He pulls from his wallet ads he's cut from *The Cross and the Stake*. One guy's offering ten thousand dollars in gold bullion.

Lyla, who's been squirming for half an hour, gets up, says, "Time to go." She hands Harry two tumblers, and he gathers up the others and takes them into the kitchen.

Marge helps Armstrong Otto into his shoes.

Harry rinses the tumblers clean, hears, over the water, Lyla say, "Harry, we'll meet you out front." The screen door slams shut.

The last thing Harry catches on the TV before he punches it off is a replay of the car dropping over the edge of the section of the Bay Bridge that fell on its lower ramp. Harry's seen the footage a hundred times. The woman driving the car is dead. And like you and me, when we've got our remote in our hand and a movie in the VCR, if Harry could, he'd rewind what he's seeing. He'd suck the car up out of the hole, freeze-frame it until he could catch a plane to San Francisco, hail a taxi, flimflam his way past cops and barricades out onto the Bay Bridge, and save the woman's life.

Lyla and Harry and Marge and Armstrong Otto walk toward Center Street. The sun has lit up the Red Hills north of town, and the cliffs are burnt orange, eerie, unreal, a drive-in movie postcard tacked to the sky. The four of them pass the new Wal-Mart that's ruined the neighborhood. It's grand opening night, and there's a sign for free helicopter rides. Kids are climbing into the chopper. Their parents stand back and wave. Harry lags behind to watch it take off. The helicopter lifts from its pad, U-turns, shudders—twhack, twhack, twhack—then seems to be pulled deeper into the sky by a cable.

Stuck's Rhonda has come to the reading, and he introduces her around. She's got carmine lips and is wearing a carmine dress, off her shoulders, puckered at the waist. She spent the day at her sister's out in Bloomington. Maybe Rhonda's twenty-seven, more like twenty-two. She's clean as a young tree and tall. Harry doubts Stuck's story about the dead husband.

The Reverend Boyd, dried pigeon shit on his suit, sidles up next to her and bows to kiss her hand when he's introduced. His tie-like-a-snake whacks her wrist.

"It bit me," she says.

Harry's mother is here safe and sound.

There's a woman playing a harp on the library's makeshift stage. She's the color of butterscotch pudding, and her dress is as fragile as tissue paper. Her hair's up, twisted into a cone, and looks as thick and scratchy as hemp. She's set a carpetbag at her feet. Her high heels have fake flowers sewn on the toes.

Stuck seats Rhonda in the front row. Harry's mother pulls The Reverend Boyd into the second row, and the others follow. The woman playing the harp stops the strings, holds them between palm and palm as if they're unruly heartbeats. She pulls a scarf from her bag, wipes her hands, and says, "My next number is 'Ten Past Two.'" Effie has come out of the wings and is watching the woman at the harp. She cuddles Poot in her arms. Armstrong Otto's holy sack sits like a miniature tent on Marge's lap. She's rolled the top tight as a cigar. Lyla keeps fingering it.

The harpist stops, and Effie shifts Poot into the crook of her arm and says, "We can't thank Saddie enough for this beautiful music." Everyone claps except Effie, who can't, because of Poot, so she nods at Saddie. Two men carry the harp to the back of the stage, and Saddie grabs her carpetbag. She carries it and her chair over and sits by the harp. Teenagers lay out a semicircle of folding chairs across the stage, and Effie introduces the readers one at a time, the Daughters of Joy and Stuck. The women wear heavy dresses, Victorian brown and black, and petticoats. It's difficult for them to sit. Each of the Daughters of Joy has on a straw bonnet and wears a string of pearls around her neck. Stuck's in top hat and tails, white gloves, and a swirling white scarf. His shoes look plastic they're so black. His vest is gray. Stuck looks slick, but he's everybody's softie.

The Daughters of Joy play with their pearls, weep, wag fingers, grieve, remonstrate, bitch and moan. Polly, Jack the Ripper's first victim, sweaty in a brown frock, says she was twelve when she married a Fleet Street printer. She sobs and talks about her five children. Sure, she was a prostitute, a whore, a chippie. They all were. But she didn't deserve what she got. None of them did. Emma, his second victim, was a widow. Did she deserve to be sliced like a cuke? Anne Chapman, whose husband was dead, took care of her crippled son. "Want to see what that fiend did to me?" She starts to undo her bodice. The other women say, "No, no." Someone in the audience says, "For heaven's sake."

Stuck ad-libs throughout, uses *hooker* fifteen different ways, then adds variations. "Hooked the wrong fish?" he says. "Fell for it hook, line, and sinker, did you?" he says. He banters with the women. Odd thing is, Effie's loving what he's doing, as if she'd counted on this. Stuck is playing Jack the Ripper as W. C. Fields. He twirls a walking stick and taps the floor after each joke, his idea of a rim shot.

Afterward, Stuck and Rhonda disappear, and Armstrong Otto keeps circling Saddie the harpist while she plays. He sets food at her feet. There's chili and crackers. Marge sticks close to Armstrong.

"Has Armstrong found one?" Harry asks Lyla. He nods toward Saddie.

Lyla says, "She's an odd color."

"The living dead, would you say?"

"She's real pasty."

"Have you seen Stuck?" Harry says.

Lyla tells him she saw Stuck and Rhonda go out the side entrance to the library.

"Do you want some chili?" Harry says to Lyla. "Or something to drink?"

"Not now," Lyla says. She heads toward Marge, but The Reverend Boyd cuts her off. His tie bounces on his belly. He's holding a bowl of chili, and Harry can't hear what he says to Lyla. Harry's mother is talking to Effie.

On the stubby porch outside the side entrance to the library, Harry leans into a railing. Stuck is over by a dumpster drinking with Rhonda and some high school kids. A streetlamp shines on them. The lighting here is '40s film noir, one polka-dot circle on the ground. Stuck has changed into cutoffs. He's barefoot and has wrapped his knees in the white elastic bandages. His tux lies like an abandoned soul across the hood of Rhonda's Cadillac. Rhonda, the only spot of color in all this black and white, holds a beer and hugs Stuck, one arm around his waist. She kisses his chin, his ear, then hickey-sucks his neck. They've balanced Dixie cups on her car. Next to them is a whiskey bottle. There are three beer bottles and a six-pack sitting on the asphalt. Stuck, smooth as Gene Kelly, twirls Rhonda aside and begins the Jack the Ripper shuffle, two-stepping to the beat of *I don't like to get up on a winter morning*. He sees Harry, tap-taps his walking stick, and says, "Are you ready for that drink yet?" He twirls the walking stick once, drops it, bends over and rests his hands on his bad knees.

"Maybe I am," Harry says. The Daughters of Joy got to Harry. All that horror. *Life,* he understands, *will, in the future and from now on, be a wretched bitch dressed in Victorian black. Fill 'em up, Bartender.* Harry hustles down the few steps and is halfway over to Stuck when he sees Stuck drop to one knee in the circle of light. It's as if he's going to sing. Al Jolson? Then Stuck collapses.

"Stuck?" Harry says.

Rhonda passes her beer to a kid and catches Stuck's shoulder. She says, "Stuck?"

Harry and Rhonda roll Stuck onto his back. One of the kids is running toward the library, and another one is headed for a phone booth on the corner. Harry's lost here. Rhonda kneels next to Harry, and she says, "What do we do?"

Whomp on his chest? Harry thinks. He's got one hand under Stuck's head.

"Clear his throat," Rhonda says.

Harry digs for Stuck's tongue. The side door to the library bangs open, and The Reverend high-jumps the porch railing. Then he's sprinting, and his snake tie is wapping him in the face. Lyla, Marge, and Armstrong Otto barge through the people who've gathered to see what's up and stand on the little square porch. Effie's next, and Poot starts barking. Saddie's still making harp music.

"What is it?" The Reverend says. He crouches on the other side of Stuck. Harry has opened Stuck's shirt. He left Stuck's tongue where it was. The Reverend squeezes Stuck's mouth into a pucker.

"Harry?" Lyla says from the porch.

It's then that Stuck opens his eyes, and he winks, only nothing on him is moving. It's like only his head is left above the quicksand he's stumbled into. He's just his two eyes crashing to earth.

Poot's gotten free and is licking Stuck's ear. The Daughters of Joy have come out and circled around like a choir. These are women Stuck taught in high school years ago when they were teenagers. Their pearls, in all this night, under the lamppost, grin, the Cheshire Cats. Poot sniffs Stuck's mouth.

"That you, Poot?" Stuck says. They'll be his last words.

From the porch, Effie says, "Poot. Harry? Poot."

Stuck's pupils flick. He closes his eyes, and then he's not breathing. Here on his neck is Rhonda's hickey, kid's stuff, the sign of boys and girls at fun in this world. Behind him, Harry hears the rustle of Armstrong Otto's holy sack. Wood knocks against wood.

The Reverend thumps Stuck's chest. He curls over Stuck, puckers up, is going to kiss life into him.

But Stuck, Stuck's a dead man, and Harry knows it.

No rising from wreckage.

No resurrection tonight.

Only Saddie's harp, the half-circle of the Daughters of Joy, and the twhack-twhack-twhack of the Wal-Mart helicopter taking kids for a joyride.

IT'S A LOT SCARIER

IF YOU TAKE JESUS OUT

Suicide, the Mormons teach you, is only a change of scenery, and it doesn't mean you can't go to heaven, just that according to their plan of salvation you spend eternity in a third-rather-than-first degree of glory, a telestial not a celestial kingdom, the celestial being the glory of the sun, even the glory of God. There was a time when I believed what the Mormons said. I was one of the youth of Zion, a standard-bearer. Friends called me Nephi, and I was good a LDS, a Latter-day Saint.

No longer. Not for years now, and not on your life.

Not since I was seventeen, when a girl named Caroline Foht-step determined in a physical way that Nephi Woods from Alpine, Utah, would be known as Woods and only Woods and in passing taught me the *x*'s and *o*'s of a snuffling post-pubescent boarding-school nihilism. "*Nee* il ism" was how she said it.

One day, at the tag end of one of our chinfests, her eloquence run dry, all our ideas and big talk kicked around and worn thin, Caroline said, "It's a lot scarier if you take Jesus out."

"People'd find a substitute," I said.

She said, "Let them."

I said, "You can't stop people."

It was one of our last powwows, our final tête-à-têtes. She went off to Berkeley, and I headed east to Princeton. We were impudent and smoking Marlboros. Our clothes were rags. I wore my hair long, up, rubberbanded, like sprouts. Hers was short as a boy's and nicked to show scalp. We were the smart kids, and our small town felt betrayed.

Now I'm thirty-one, living again in Alpine, Utah, and if the Mormons are right I can't abide the law of either the celestial or terrestrial glory. I'm bound for the telestial.

So is an ex-girlfriend, Jill, who took her own life yesterday.

To do so is to break the law.

My sin? I denied my birthright, my God. I said no-thanks to the Mormons and their ways and broke my family's heart.

The two of us, Jill and I, we chose, in different ways, to become a law unto ourselves. We shall not, when the resurrection of the dead comes, dwell in God's presence. We will not be of the Church of the Firstborn, and our hell will be in knowing what we could have had. Still, all is not lost. Even the glory of the telestial is a glory that surpasses in its beauty all understanding.

Stuart, who lived in the same house in the studio apartment across from Jill, phoned me about her. "I have the worst news," he began. When he hung up, I speed-dialed Jill and her machine answered. "Hello," her recording said. "It's almost eight o'clock, and I'm going out for the evening. Goodbye." That was the lie to end all lies, wasn't it? "Goodbye" could mean a hundred different things. Jill killed herself sometime in the hours of stubborn thought that come just before the sun rises. She drove into Lambs Canyon east of Salt Lake City, ran a hose from her exhaust into her car, and rolled up the windows.

I begged off when Stuart said friends were getting together to talk.

Jill and I once lived together for three years in Salt Lake. I held her hand while she aborted one child. We kept birds. Chin Up and Chin Down, we called them. One summer in Yellowstone, canoeing in country even God has forgotten he created, we saw a moose fight another moose.

So one night I slept, Jill died, and I woke and drove to my office not knowing she had. Utah's economy is off the charts, and I broker whatever you want brokered and make good money. On the way home I stopped at the market, picked up Honey Wheat bread, and bought Coca-Cola magnets I stuck to my refrigerator. I opened the windows at the rear of my third-floor apartment, turned on the TV, and read the mail, all as if I could stop what I was doing at any minute, phone Jill, and say, "What's up?" She lived in Park City, forty minutes away.

Then it was 3 A.M., and sitting on the sofa, having nipped at the same tumbler of bourbon for hours, blindsided by Stuart's phone call, I noticed the shirt I was wearing had lost a button, the top one closest to my neck.

Mind-boggling, right?

Suicide. A lost button. Go tell it on a mountaintop.

TNT was showing *Dr. Phibes Rises Again*, Vincent Price, blood-shot and glassy-eyed, vamping himself. You hear people say *My heart's in my throat.* Mine was. On the phone, Stuart said, "A family found her."

I settled the tumbler of bourbon into the carpet at my feet. It had lost its kick, could have been piss at that point. Engage yourself, I thought. Mind the store. Don't idle. Don't loaf. Put one foot in front of the other. Move. So I did. In my closet I collected five more shirts that had lost buttons. I searched through the laundry basket. Three shirts, no missing buttons. Keep busy, that's unofficial Mormon doctrine. Utah's state emblem is a beehive. Worker bees, that's the idea. The idler is, as everyone knows, the devil's. I took off the shirt I was wearing and piled all six on a chair next to the front door.

The Yellow Pages listed Cloth Etc. under Sewing. It was the middle of the night, but I dialed the number anyway. The store was located in a strip mall nearby, ten minutes away, half an hour if I walked. The shop's machine answered, a woman's voice telling me the hours. Everybody on planet earth, even me, even Woods, knows that when you sew you take the thread to the needle, not the needle to the thread. Somehow you understand that. You kitty-corner your stitches on buttons. Still, I would need hints, pointers, guidance. How, for example, do you keep the button loose enough so you can work it through its hole? I hoped someone at Cloth Etc. could help, like the pro in an auto parts store, the guy who tells you the '86 Mercury Cougar doesn't use the alternator the '83 through '85 Cougar uses.

I opened more windows in my apartment and searched the screens for tears, then poured fresh bourbon, two fingers. The night was hot for October. In the fields behind my place, a witches' moon backgrounded the apple orchard. Over the past three weeks, pickers had stripped the trees and pruned them. All day, men and boys had climbed around like kids out of school. By each tree, they left a bundle of limbs.

I speed-dialed Jill again and listened to her voice. She said, "Hello. It's almost eight o'clock, and I'm going out for the evening. Goodbye."

"Goodbye" could mean anything.

Cloth Etc. seemed empty. Then someone in the back fired up a vacuum. The store was as big as an auditorium. Bolts of cloth stood upright on display tables shoved together in rows, fabric pinned up and into wings as if it was trying to fly. In a corner near the front was a sewing shop, five Singers in a half circle, scraps of material and tissue paper on the floor, flimsy patterns thumbtacked to corkboard. Somebody had abandoned cloth in one of the machines.

A boy hurried around a partition and began vacuuming behind the cash register. He'd hooked a Walkman to his belt, and it connected to earphones.

Lydia, the woman I date, told me I wanted tortoiseshell buttons. On my way out this morning, I knocked on her door. She lives in the red-tiled Spanish-looking complex next to mine. Lydia picked through the shirts I was carrying and said, "They're all tortoiseshell."

I said, "Can you come with me?"

"Not today."

"It's Saturday," I said.

She told me she was catching up on work.

I said, "Not for love or money or a good time?"

"Another day," Lydia said. "Another time, sure, if you can hold off I'll go with you."

I held up the shirts.

She said, "Is there some rush?"

"Just doing errands," I said.

She said, "How long have those shirts been without buttons?"

"I don't know."

"Then you can wait."

I shrugged, said, "They're on my mind."

"You don't need to drag the shirts along," Lydia said. "The buttons are all the same."

I said, "See how much I need your help."

She said, "Just a minute," and went into her bedroom. She

came back, handed me a tortoiseshell button, and took the shirts. "I'll be here when you're done," she said. "Pick up the shirts and have a swim." Her landlord had told her he was draining the pool on Monday. He'd said, "Weather's coming." Lydia showed me the cartoon she was roughing in, one of a haggard woman standing on a lawn, a For Sale sign next to this tired old bag who was calling out to a man wearing only boxer shorts. The man had his pants and shirt folded over his arm. His shoes dangled from his hand, and he was tiptoeing away. The woman was saying, "Wait. You've got another think coming." I didn't get the joke, and Lydia could tell. She said, "Trust me. It'll tickle your funny bone when I'm finished."

Her cartoons do. They're syndicated. You probably look for them yourself. People tack them to bulletin boards and tape them to office doors. They Xerox them and mail copies to relatives. They fax them to friends. Odds are you've done it.

I told Lydia about Jill, and she said, "I'm sorry. That's awful, no matter how you look at it."

Lydia knew Jill and I had lived together. Soon after she and I started going out, she heard a message on my machine, Jill saying, "Woods, this is Jill, from before." Jill had called to say she'd moved back to Salt Lake City.

Along two walls of Cloth Etc. hung rows of buttons on white cards, arranged according to someone's logic, but I couldn't figure it out. I pulled free a set and compared the buttons to the one Lydia gave me. Right idea, only too big. Row after row I squinted and touched and measured and didn't find what I was after.

Behind me, to my left, the vacuum stopped. I turned around, and the boy said, "The women are both gone."

I asked if the place was open.

He said, "They went for yogurt."

He'd come in close enough that I showed him the tortoiseshell button Lydia gave me, and he rolled his head, humped the wires that led to his earphones into a loop. "You seen any of these?" I said. He lowered the volume on his radio, and I said, "Could there be some buttons not on the wall? Maybe in some drawers?"

"I just clean the place mornings and Saturdays," he said. "Probably."

The kid was more helpless than I was. "I'll keep hunting," I said.

He said, "They'll be back," and clicked on his vacuum, U-turned up an aisle, and rolled past bolts of cloth.

You bought needles in packets of ten or fifteen, sized from short and thin to long and thick. I couldn't see any way to buy just one. I found the buttons I needed on a sale table. They came in plastic boxes of twenty-five. The women had not come back, the boy knew nothing, and I didn't want to haggle, so I added up the cost of what I owed and put my money on the counter next to the cash register.

Outside I stayed with the mall sidewalk and wandered into a couple of shops. I was after an ashtray, something gimmicky about it. Lydia collected them. She owns a clay ashtray that speaks to you, that says, "Hey, Butt Face," when you stump out your cigarette. One she has is a rowboat. You rest your cigarette where an oar would go. I stopped outside a western store where the boots were half off. A sign said THIS IS THE PLACE WHERE FASHION MEETS THE WEST.

Two women coming toward me were eating yogurt. One wore a scarf on her head. They got close, and I said, "Do you work at the cloth shop?" The woman wearing the scarf turned her plastic spoon upside down so she could stick me in the eye if I took one step toward them. The other woman said, "Yes, we do." Her hair was the color of dark fudge, and she'd had it cut to her shoulders. She lifted it clear on one side and wedged the hair behind her ear, then did the other side, as if we'd met at a party and she was going to hear me out.

I dug the thread and buttons out of my jacket, showed them in my open hand, and said, "I came in and got these and put the money on the counter."

"We've been buying yogurt," she said and showed me her cup. "No one has been in all morning." Her yogurt was chocolate, walnut and mint sprinkled on top. She said, "That was good of you. We got carried away, window-shopping."

I told her I didn't know what the tax was, and she said, "The machine does that."

I said, "I added a dollar."

"We'll call it even," she said. "How's that?"

"The boy didn't seem to know much."

"He doesn't," she said, and the two women walked around me. A braid lying between the shoulders of the woman in the scarf fanned out at its end like the tip of a paintbrush. She wore high heels, and a silver hoop the size of a quarter swung from one ear. She turned and stared at me, as if she might one day need to identify this weirdo to the police.

I waited a few minutes and then went back to Cloth Etc. The boy came out the door, unchained a bicycle from a rack, and pedaled toward the street. Through the storefront eaves-to-ground windows, I saw the woman who had talked to me. Something about her, maybe her hair, made me think of Jill. She stood at the cash register. My guess was she was ringing up the money I'd left. She hesitated as if someone had called her name and then quickly twisted around and looked directly at me. I stepped back, sensed the edge of the sidewalk at my heels, and in a flash what was reflected in the window—a trick of light, depth and shadow and plate glass—was me and behind me in the parking lot Jill.

I stumbled through a box step, trying to catch a glimpse.

No Jill. Of course not. In fact, no one.

Jill perfected two acts, her Old World mother routine and her Mona Lisa. What I saw in the window was the Old World mother, a shrug for this and a shrug for that and the air full of her words and her hands. Jill did enough talking for three lifetimes, but not enough shrugging or talking to defend taking your own life. No one's entitled. Shrug and talk till you're blue in the face. They say it's the one choice we can make. Screw anyone who says so.

From inside, at the register, the woman beckoned me. I touched my chest, saying, *Me?* Thinking, *You want Woods?*

She waved me in.

"I can't find any money," she said.

I touched the spot where I'd laid the cash, rubbed the countertop, and said, "A five and three ones."

She stepped back, surveyed the area.

"How about under the register?" I said. I helped her tilt it so we could see. Nothing. She ran a yardstick underneath it. Nothing.

"Right here," I said, and I patted the counter.

I'd come back to Cloth Etc. We needed common sense to rule. Would a thief come back? I was not a liar, not for eight dollars' worth of sewing supplies. In the movies, fire bugs, serial killers, and mad bombers return to the scene of the crime, but would a notions thief want to see the aftermath? I got out my wallet and said, "I put it in plain sight." I hoped she'd bring up the boy. I emptied my pockets, the thread, the buttons, the needles. I handed over a ten and said, "Do I have to buy a full box of buttons?"

"Of these, you do," she said and stopped tapping in prices.

I said it was okay.

She said, "We keep a jar of all kinds of buttons if you want to go through it."

"I'll take the box," I said, and I offered my business card, saying, "If you find the other money, let me know." I circled both of my phone numbers, home and office. I said, "It's not the amount. That's not it."

She said, "Would you like a sack?"

The woman in the scarf was never more than ten feet away, reconnoitering, acting like she was counting stock, taking inventory.

I said to the woman who'd helped me, "Are you married?"

"I'm a married woman," she said.

"I just thought I'd ask."

She handed me my change and said, "It's a compliment, your asking. It's nice."

Outside, I couldn't remember where I'd parked. In my head I was playing the day's music backward and at the wrong speed. It shouldn't have been as hot as it was, not in October. I held the sack against the sun and looked over the cars.

The bodies of the resurrected shall be quickened in their glory, which is celestial. In addition to those who lived righteously, to those who kept God's commandments on earth there will be two kinds of spirits in heaven, in the celestial kingdom, in that highest degree of glory. There will be the angels, who have bodies of flesh and bone, and there will be the spirits of the just, who have not been resurrected but who have inherited the same glory, angels in the company of angels, among those of the Church of the First Born.

The gospel. It's the good news, they say.

Jill was cremated. Her wish.

One of Caroline Fohtstep's ongoing jokes was to wonder if God, in all his omnipotence and wisdom, could have put Humpty Dumpty back together again.

In the face of her IQ, I wasn't about to say, "I bet he could."

I'd been with Jill when she got her donor's card. She made a point of doing this, didn't just say yes when she renewed her driver's license. We went to a local hospital, and they gave us one of those Q&A pamphlets, *How to Make the Contribution of a Lifetime*. The first Q was: *Who can become a donor and what can be donated?* A: *Anyone*. Organs include kidneys, hearts, lung, liver, pancreas. Tissue include corneas, skin, bone, middle ear, blood vessels, tendons, heart valves. One other Q stuck: *What if I change my mind about donating?* The A was: *Just tear up your card.*

These days, movie and TV stars, usually the ones who play doctors, they do TV ads. There is life after death, they say. Share your life. Share your decision.

Other ads say, Pass on hope.

It occurs to me that somewhere in this wide country of ours Jill's heart could be pumping someone's blood, and someone could be seeing through Jill's eyes. Her kidney could be doing its cleaning for a stranger.

Is all that really possible? Not simply theory?

Lydia and I arrived late to the memorial service. *So*, Jill would have said, *Woods being late, this is news? What, am I to telephone people? The press? Should I wire NBC?*

Her Old-World mother routine.

Followed by her Mona Lisa, that smile.

A drowsy old man stopped us in the foyer, said, "Shhhhh," and put a finger to his lips. He looked wormy. He was wearing tennis shoes and half glasses. He said to me, "It's almost over."

Lydia and I stepped into an alcove. She'd worn black and pearls, one strand, high-class. Jill's brother, when we introduced ourselves, said, "So you're Woods." At least he'd heard of me. Three years I'd lived with Jill and I'd never met her family. Had not once talked to them on a phone. Her father rocked on his feet near an exit, as if he'd been paid to be here, and her mother hugged me loosely, as if I had a disease. She said, "You were one of Jill's friends." They'd flown in from Miami.

I nodded, claimed I'd been a good friend.

"So many friends," her mother said.

We stood close to a table of food, and Lydia held my arm. I felt the way I used to feel at high school dances. Can't waltz or two-step, and won't try, and everything about me says, *Don't ask*. I was the only person at the funeral in brown shoes.

Outside, getting in the car, Lydia said, "Maybe she is happy where she is."

I let her stupidity go until I'd started the engine. Then I said, "Do people still talk that way?"

She said, "Some of us do."

"You're talking about heaven and hell?" I said.

She said, "Whatever you want to call it. An afterlife. A better place. You don't believe in it, and I do. It's disagreement that makes the world go round."

So I quoted Caroline Fohtstep. "It's a lot scarier," I said, "if you take Jesus out."

Lydia said, "We don't just disappear."

"What do we do?" I said.

"Whatever it is," she said, "we don't go poof into nothing."

I eased the Mazda around the corner and saw Jill's father standing in an alley by a side entrance to the mortuary. He was a squat old guy, a frog on a lily pad. He plugged a cigar into his mouth. I caught a movement out of the corner of my eye and glanced up to see a curtain drop back into place in a second-story window of the mortuary. Jill, I thought. She couldn't stay away. She had to check out who came and hear what was said.

I left Lydia at her place and drove west, away from our apartments, toward Utah Lake, then the desert. I didn't want to drive into the canyons or the mountains. When I got back, I dialed Jill, and a man answered. If I'd said, *Is Jill there?* he'd have said, *Jill passed away.* Or equivalent drivel. I could have gotten pushy and said, *Who is this?* like I was the jealous lover. I could have been angry and said, *What are you doing at Jill's place?* I could have been sly and said, *I'd like to leave a message for Jill.*

Irritated, the man said, "Hello?" It was not her father, and it wasn't her brother.

I said, "Jill?"

"Jill's dead," the man said.

I held the phone to my ear until he hung up. What else could I have done?

From my office, the day after the service, I phoned Cloth Etc. and asked for the woman with the dark hair. I said, "I was in the other day, and she helped me."

The woman who answered—the one who was wearing the scarf, no doubt—said, "Just a minute."

I jammed the instep of my loafer against my desk's open bottom drawer and committed myself to a pair of boots at that store *where fashion meets the West.* I'd buy black on black.

"Good morning," the woman said.

I said, "I'm the one who bought the thread and buttons and left the money on the counter."

"We thought so," she said.

"You sound lovely," I said.

"Thank you."

I said, "You sound like you've got a dozen roses sitting there on the counter in front of you."

"I don't see any roses," she said.

I said, "But you can imagine them?"

"I can."

I said, "Did you find the money?"

"Not yet."

"Maybe it will show up," I said. "I did leave it, Boy Scout's honor."

She said, "I hope so."

I said, "Do you mind if I ask your name?"

"Arnette."

"I've never heard that one before."

"It comes from my family," she said. "It was my grandmother's name, for one, and an aunt along the way."

I said, "It's nice. I like it."

"Another compliment," she said.

So I was the compliment man. She remembered, and foolish man that I am I was proud because she had. I said, "What about the boy? Is he a possibility?"

"A possibility?"

"He was there vacuuming. He could have taken the money, don't you think?"

She said, "Was he here?"

"He was in the store when I left."

"Then he could have."

"I don't want to accuse him," I said. "He seemed nice, but he was taking off on his bicycle when I came back. Didn't you see him?"

"If he was here, it's a possibility."

I said, "I don't know if he even noticed me put the money on the counter. He was in the back someplace. But he could have. Or he might have seen it on his way out."

"Maybe."

"It was in plain sight."

She said, "By the register."

"Right by the register," I said. "On the counter where I showed you." I sat up, said, "He seemed honest."

"I think he is," she said. "He's my son."

I said, "I didn't mean—"

"No," she said, "it's okay. He was here, and you put your money on the counter where anyone could see it. He's a teenager, and who knows why teenagers do what they do."

"I know I did some wild things when I was a kid," I said. This got no response. No "Me, too." Or "Didn't we all." I imagined her pretty mouth in a frown. I said, "Arnette, are you still married this afternoon?"

"This afternoon, I am," she said. "Yes."

"Would you want a yogurt when you get off?"

"One more compliment," she said.

I said, "I have more, if you'll meet me. I'm full of compliments. They're like magic with me."

She said, "If I want yogurt with someone, I'll ask my husband. He's a good sport."

Tonight, I'm sewing buttons on my shirts, and Lydia is here for company. I've finished two collars, and when I button them they're knock-kneed. Our subject, over country music, Reba McEntire, is Jill. Lydia wonders what she was to me. This is adult conversation. There is no jealousy here.

"Not much of a friend when I really knew her," I say.

Lydia says, "Lovers but not friends." Her mouth, I realize for the first time, is the one I see on the female characters in her cartoons. It's not as pretty as Jill's or the woman's at Cloth Etc., but it can cast a spell.

Jill and I *were* lovers but not friends. We were a cliché, at best. She talked, and I listened. She had ways she used to cut me off. Her eyes said she didn't want to hear certain things. They said, *Shut up.* I say to Lydia, "That's what we were."

After Lydia heard Jill say on my machine, "Woods, this is Jill, from before," she never called me Woods again. To Lydia, I'm Nephi.

Lydia gets up and goes to the refrigerator. "Anything to drink?" she says.

The subject of Jill is gone, has passed, like one of those every-one-hundred-year comets. I want to explain how sad we'd been as lovers even though I know I'd be singing an old song, so I follow Lydia to the refrigerator. She gets a mineral water and offers me a bottle. I pass.

Lydia sets her water aside, puts her hands on my shoulders, and says, "I'm sorry about Jill."

"Me, too," I say.

She says, "I've got to go. Work calls."

I toss my shirts in a closet. Who bothers with shirts that don't have buttons? You just don't wear them, or you take them somewhere. Maybe to a place like Cloth Etc. I'm tempted to tell Lydia that Jill made me go bowling—her league average was 160—and she took me to the Bachauer piano competition one night. I rented a tux, totally unnecessary, given the Salt Lake City crowd. Jill sat with her chin on the seat in front of us. Didn't say one word. Not all night. She fell in love with one of the contestants and wrote him long letters. We'd be in a room together at our place, and she'd be writing this guy, asking me how to word a sentence. "Is that too obvious?" she'd ask, like we were girlfriends talking about her new crush. The man never answered her letters. We'd be in a room together and she'd be trying to call him.

At the door, Lydia says, "Planetary factors, the sensational aspect between the sun in Pisces and Jupiter in Cancer, will give you peace. You've had your fill of broken promises, and what occurs will serve to set you free."

"You just made that up," I said.

"Even so," she said, "it's true."

Sometimes I appear in Lydia's cartoons. I'm an ongoing character, a paleontologist who returns now and then from godforsaken regions carrying fossils I've dug up. I wear a leather coat like one I've told Lydia I want to own, one of those fleece-lined flyer's jackets, only the coat she draws me in has dinosaur tracks climbing up the back of it and running down the front. I have beady eyes and a potato nose. I wear a cap, its bill curled.

Lydia's gone, it's going on 4 A.M., and I've downed three tumblers of bourbon when I take the footpath into the orchard. Step after step, I see my breath, smell the liquor I've had. The moon has stiffened. I'm carrying my buttonless shirts and matches. My plan is I'm going to light a pile of limbs on fire and burn the shirts. I've thought about this. Out of sight out of mind is my thinking. But it's freezing. The weather Lydia's landlord said was coming is here. Since sunset, October has turned on us. I cram myself into one shirt, then another one. Low branches jab at me. They cut my arms and my face. Crossing an irrigation ditch, I twist my left ankle, stumble, and twist my right ankle. I sit on the bank to rub them, and an owl hoots. I've sat in mud.

What Jill did was beyond calculated. There was the phone message, no "After the beep, tell me who you are and I'll get back to you," only her message and "Goodbye." What's that? She knew I'd call, was betting I'd need to hear her voice. I yank two more shirts on and roll the others around my hands as a muff. The shirts I'm wearing are bulky. I'll end up sick. Someone's hauled away the tree trimmings the pickers left behind, so there'll be no lighting a fire, no burning the shirts unless I break off limbs. Which is okay. I need every stitch of clothing I've got. I rest against a tree trunk, huddle myself into myself.

There's a harvest moon. So bright it casts shadows.

Jill was alive one second and then gone. It must be like surgery. Count backward from one hundred, and you never get past ninety-nine.

Was she cold?

Like me, here? I hope and pray not.

I do manage a small fire using twigs and grass I can clump together, and I sit for hours in the orchard, and then I'm up and walking. By sunrise, I'm roaming the walkway in front of Cloth Etc. I've lost a shoe in mud, and I've put all but one shirt on. It's wrapped around my hands. The others tug at me. My arms and legs feel stubby, as if they've been fattened and foreshortened. I could be the guy police dogs practice on.

There's hoarfrost on the pavement.

A couple of cars in the parking lot look frozen. The boy who cleans the shop wheels past, slows down, then circles around. He hops off his bicycle and chains it to a pole. He's wearing a parka and gloves. He says, "Hey," and struts by, fitting his Walkman to his pants. It could snow. The air sparkles where the morning sunlight hits it. That's how cold it's turned. My foot hurts, so I sit on the curbing. I bundle my last shirt around the foot, and I wonder if I could lose some toes. The sky is sinking, and I'm tall enough, if I could do what's necessary to get off my butt and onto my feet, I could touch it. It's low. Maybe I could keep it in its place.

The two women from Cloth Etc. drive by and park near the edge of the lot, close to the street. Once they're out of the car, they see me, and the one who was ready to spoon me to death zips open her handbag. She's got Mace, and she is—I can see this clearly—in an unfinished-business sense pleased that I've shown up. The look in her eye is Caroline Fohtstep's. Caroline liked both fire and ice. When you're seventeen, you've got the world by the tail.

Me? I'm Lydia's beady-eyed paleontologist. I'm back from Mongolia, the Gobi Desert, carrying fossils and the truth about Brontosaurus. I haven't had time to shower. I have proof that old thunder lizard is not Apatosaurus, the deceptive lizard. Even if it's only a cartoon, I have evidence.

Caroline—I almost say this out loud—the substitute is here. I understand what I look like. I'm the bogeyman. I stink, and you could peel the shirts from me like scabs. I'm bad news. Your reason for worrying about me is justified. I've lost a shoe. I'm the killer in the slasher film. Just when the townsfolk begin to celebrate the fact that they've taken care of me once and for all, when I've been buckshot, bludgeoned, chained, and sent packing, when I've been set on fire and dynamited, when I've been squashed in the car crusher, the music swells and I lurch to my feet, unfold myself limb by limb. I'm cut and bruised and worse off for all they've done to me, but I'm alive.

Rejoice is what I have to say.

There is life after death. The Resurrection is literal.

The woman gives me Caroline Fhotstep's hawk eye and aims her Mace at me, and the other woman, the one I've talked to, Arnette, straightens her arms in a way that Jill used to, as if she's launching a boat, and she says, "Stay where you are."

That's fine with me.

With her free hand, the woman with Mace has flipped open a cell phone, and she's dialing 911. Inside, the kid's dialing 911. People in cars driving by, they're dialing 911. The woman says, "Don't move."

As if I am planning to.

Y ou got older. You got opinions," Plugg said. He talked that way. Like an after-dinner speaker. Like he was celibate. We were shooting pool, nine ball. He'd run the table on me, and I was racking next game. He said, "So life goes. Step two builds on step one." He built steps in the air, said, "You climb so high you're looking down like one of those spaceship photos. It happens, and the world comes into being. You were a kid. Now you express yourself stubbornly and without reservation. Now you call your own press conferences." Plugg talked like Judgment Day. He claimed he'd read Plato. Aristotle. Knew how to make a point, how the A's, B's, and C's fit together, how to use upper and lowercase Roman numerals, their backstitching and tuck and roll, their this-in-support-of-that format. Their one-hand-washes-the-other geometry.

I'd one minute earlier told Plugg that Hector Macho Camacho was going to dismantle Sugar Ray Leonard and toss Sugar's leftovers in a body bag. I said the fight wouldn't go two rounds. I joked that Sugar Ray couldn't run fast enough. I had gone so far as to refer to Sugar Ray as geriatric and a windbag. I said, "He's forty and in great shape, great shape for forty, which is like the one about Lincoln. *Other than that, Mrs. Lincoln, how did you like the play?*" I read in the *Las Vegas Sun* where Sugar Ray is telling reporters he wants to get it over with and go home. Is that fighter talk? Not in my book. It's embarrassing he's talking like that. I'd said to Plugg, "Do the math. Forty isn't twenty." I said, "The bloom is off the rose." I do my own reading. Poetry, if you must know.

I broke our next rack, weak as always, nothing dropped. The good news was I left Plugg buried and with a table I didn't mind giving up, balls clustered like plastic fruit. We traded safeties until I let the cue ball loose off a rail. Plugg, not even glancing my way, frozen in that five-hundred-year-old snooker stance of his, his stick alongside his cheek and brushing the necktie he'd wear into the twenty-first century, should he live that long, he said, "We get you a bout and we got an event people will bet on."

I said, "That's not happening."

"It'd be an afternoon card, is all," Plugg said. "Upside is it's at Caesar's. The downside is it's not the ballroom. Upside, it's televised and you get purse and percentage. Pronto bucks. You arguing you can't use the money?"

"I can't use the money."

"You farting in silk these days?" he said, knocking home the three, his cue ball trailing it like a puppy, then softly smooching the rail and coming off it before settling in position on the four. He sank the four and five, said, "I've negotiated somewhat with people who can put this together." He froze the cue ball on the six, had the seven in his sights.

Translated, negotiated means *dicked around.*

Plugg said, "Sanchez, Augie Sanchez, is this a name you've heard?"

"I know Papa Sanchez."

"His dad."

"I've seen Augie around."

"For one reason, he's hometown. For a second reason, you're hometown. You're a big puncher. They say he's a big puncher. Likes to brawl. He wants Mayweather and the title."

"So he needs some walkovers."

"You see yourself as a walkover?"

I said, "I don't need to. He can have Mayweather."

"You think I'm pouring piss in your ear?" Plugg said.

I said, "I think I don't need this."

"Sure," Plugg said, "you got roofs to roof."

First words I ever heard out of the mouth of the man I'd learn to call Plugg were, "You got hands palookas ten years older and light-years more desperate than you would kill for." I was fifteen. Plugg had hotfooted it two rows at a time down the mostly empty bleachers at the City Rec on Bonanza, Las Vegas, Nevada, and stopped me mid-dribble of a three-on-one fast break. It was a weekday afternoon, summer, the building full of echoes. Crossing half court, I stripped clean a kid nicknamed Skippy, last year's all-league point guard, and me and my posse, we skedaddled the other way, some kind of basket-rattling dunk waiting on us. This was gym-rat ball, call your own fouls.

There in front of me stood Plugg. Carl Thomas Plugg, his real name. Two g's, as in Kellogg.

Palooka floored me both as word and as sound, the vocabulary, I recognized, of my tribe.

"My name's Plugg," Plugg said, me thinking New York, New York, audacity and accent. Single-minded greed and avidity. Words I didn't have at the time, and wouldn't until I became the reader I now am. There on the hardwood was Plugg. Contemptuous, some lust. Cagey. Vice. "Show me your feet," Plugg said.

His manner of dress was Old World snazzy, hat in hand, vest, heavy pleated trousers, hand-painted silk tie. Fustian charm. He wore a mustache.

Fifteen, as I said, brain on idle while my body fed and grew on its appetites, which amounted to girls who spit in the open and wore boots, McDonald's, and enough beer to uphold my position in the community of delinquents I ran with, not one solid fact or theorem in my head, I accommodated Plugg and showed him my feet, my footwork, which led to my taking up first silver and then golden gloves and finally turning pro until I came to the tragic understanding that my hands, the one's palookas would kill for, could beat other men beyond repair.

You do this once, you harm a man, and you can beg forgiveness. Twice, and you need to look inside yourself. Check for miswiring.

Do you understand real harm?

Say it. Say the word *harm*.

Do you understand what it means?

You don't.

Trust me on this.

What's the story on Plugg and me? Ours was a union because I was the talent he spotted, and I fulfilled my promise, climbed in the ring for my first bout and left a southpaw like he'd been tossed from the ceiling above us to the canvas below. Next, a series of small-fries, and then I embarrassed an Olympic hopeful during an Olympic year. Later, I stopped the flyweight champ two steps out of his corner. A day after, he still couldn't see. Can he now? Plugg said, "Don't ask," and seven years later, I don't. I hear rumors around the city.

Harm.

You know how they say to say a word until it's not a word.

Try it. Say *harm* one thousand times.

Harm. Harm. Harm. Harm. Harm.

That game don't work.

Quick hands are one thing. Quick hands that strike like Cadillacs, quick hands that run red lights—they're the horror your artists write about. Take one, Mr. Norman Mailer, who I read on the way to becoming the educated man I am to date here in the entertainment capital of the world. Mr. Mailer holds himself and speaks like he knows boxing. *Prizefighter* is a word he uses. *Pugilist.* Uses with purpose. Words, they matter to Mr. Norman Mailer. He has his reasons. Everyone does, they tell us. Mr. Norman Mailer can't differentiate his ass from his ear hole. Ask on the back streets where no one b.s.'s.

You can't know what it's like to hit. Here, do this. Get yourself up to full speed running downhill, at night, when it's pitch-black, no moon, no streetlights, and, aware its in front of you at the bottom of the hill, run yourself smack into a brick wall. You've acquainted yourself with my jab. Don't even think about my overhand right. I get inside and hook. I get inside and blast, ambidextrously. Mr. Norman Mailer, he got in the ring in the Navy, was it? Am I remembering right? Maybe it was the Marines. No difference I can tell.

Words aren't fists, no matter how you argue it. The pen is not mightier than the sword, or however that goes.

Here's fact, ice-pick true. Women admire brutality, even the sweet ones, your sisters and your mothers. Your wives. The ones who whisper in your ears. They cover their eyes and peek through their fingers. Study their mouths. You'll find no mercy there.

Try this. Squat-walk a mile and you'll understand the strength in my legs, which is where your power resides and which is what gives you the wherewithal to slip a punch.

So I moved up a weight class, eventually leaving its belt holder, Hurricane Dominquez, deaf and dumb. He can't recall his own name. His eyes don't focus. They float in their sockets. Hurricane won't ever work, not in this lifetime.

Am I bragging? I don't mean to.

What happened happened.

I'm a realist who gave better than he took. My glass has water in it. That's all. It's not half empty, and it's not half full. I banged, and I'll admit I ate too many punches. Liked to brawl. Was proud of my chin.

No one I knew could duck and hide a cue ball or organize a table like Plugg. Over fifty, eyes no longer a kid's, and he still gave you the breaks and the five ball and ended up wearing your overcoat and lacing your brand-new three-hundred-dollar boots on his feet.

This what I'm telling you is about me at twenty-seven and Plugg at fifty-three. For something to do, I roofed days and shot pool at night. I had plenty of money. A palooka I was, but smart, like in the ant and the fable. I invested and bought land. This is about me letting Plugg down. Maybe, like he was claiming, his bankroll had gone into my going into the ring one more time. I wasn't about to accommodate him. Not, as they say, for love or spite. You know how some boys hook up with someone other than their father. I'd done that with Plugg. Not because I didn't have a father. I did, still do, one solid to the core, and a mother, though she's dead of illness a few months now. Both of them good people with backbone.

They never saw me fight. My mother's, Edna's, decision.

"I make this, you go back in the ring," Plugg said. "I'm taking the back road," he said. He meant he'd bank the shot. He had me seven-zip, nine ball, my day's pay in cash on the lamp shade above the table, already on its way to Plugg's wallet. He had a five-nine combination waiting the bank he'd left himself on the four ball.

That squat walk I mentioned before, do it once across an 8-12 pitched roof and you'll understand the kind of shape I was still in, and you'll appreciate Plugg's urgency. "My money's yours fair and square," I said. "I'm not."

"Like I say," Plugg said. "You're young, you got your fists and the way you wear your clothes. You add a few years, and now it's talk is what you do." He swept his hands over his attire, then set himself above his right knee, laced his cue stick between his fingers, and said, "Disappointment piles up." His stick brushed his tie. "It sorrows me. You lower your threshold," he said. "You quit sending food back. The waiter plops shit on your plate, which, by the way, is cracked, and you fork it down. Who are you to be offending? Should the offended offend? Where would it stop, all this offending?" Plugg housed the four, called the five-nine and nailed it. He straightened up, stretched his back, and said, "One more time around the block. Not for money but on the up-and-up for you."

"I don't play for me," I said.

"One bout."

I stood pat.

He said, "Bounce pool."

He'd insulted me. Bounce pool is bank pool, nothing but bank shots. It's a sucker's game.

He said, "I play southpaw."

More insult.

I said, "Another hundred, and not for me. We shoot straight up, not bounce, not lefty."

Plugg took the original stake from the light above the table, pocketed my one hundred, my five twenties. I dug balls out of their pockets. "I'll get the table," he said. We'd occupied a back room for two hours plus, twenty bucks an hour. "I mean no disrespect," he said.

He did, of course, mean disrespect. Loser paid. Pool is not a game of generosity. Pool players, the real ones, gentlemen or ladies, you give them a shot and they'll stick the rack down your throat and use your money to buy the liquor to help the balls go down easier.

Next morning, Sunday, I ran a slow two miles to Golden Gloves Gym on Charleston, did some bag work, and floated through a couple of rounds with a cabby pal we call U-turn, for his driving, yes, but more for the route his left hook takes. You could surgically remove his heart and sew up his chest in the time it took him to land one of those roundhouses. U-turn offered me a lift home. I wanted to jump rope, and I needed more miles on the road. "Next time," I said.

Noon I drove out to my dad's. He'd built a place at Seven Hills in Henderson, half an acre lot, gated neighborhood. My kid sister, Ginger, sixteen, lived with him. She was sitting on the steps of dad's front porch, getting sun. The porch spread itself across the front of the house. It was tiled, and a low stucco fence enclosed it. Every ten feet or so he'd set terra-cotta planters as big as garbage cans. They contained some kind of flowering cactus. I parked on the street, got out, came and stood below Ginger.

She said, "Nuts," her fingers at her ear. "Should be healed," she said. She ran a finger around the edge of her ear.

I said, "How long has it been?"

She'd had a third hole pierced in her left ear, this one dead center at the top. She said, "Longer than you'd think." She stroked her ear like it was a dog's, said, "Nuts."

"You don't need me to tell you to keep it clean," I said. "Have you been using alcohol on it?"

She said, "I'm not retarded."

I said, "Gus is here, I guess."

She said, "So, what do you think if I change my name to Paisley?"

"Paisley's a stupid name."

"Yeah, so what do you think?"

"Why?"

"Too many Gingers."

"It'll pass," I said.

Her boyfriend, a kid named Snyder—that's his first name—turned the corner, tires squealing on the hot street, and Ginger gave me her hand so I could help her to her feet. I examined her ear. It was red, and it hurt her where I touched. "Something's not right," I said.

She said, "Duh."

Snyder coasted into the driveway, cut the engine on his '65 Mustang, and hopped out, saying, "I heard you're going to fight."

"You heard wrong," I said.

He said, "No?"

Ginger hugged him. "Snyder, let's go," she said, and she headed for his car.

Snyder said to me, "So you're not fighting?"

Gus, my dad, came out the front door, his left hand up in a salute, shading his eyes against the sun. "I hear you're fighting again," he said.

Ginger leaned inside Snyder's car and honked the horn. I said to Snyder, "Run her by Mecham's and have him look at that ear." Mecham was a retired doctor who lived down the street. He sewed me together more than once when I was a kid and we all lived in our old neighborhood.

Gus said, "Do that, Snyder. Will you?"

"You think she needs to?" Snyder said.

I said, "If she's smart and doesn't want that ear to fall off in her hand."

Snyder opened his door and Ginger hopped in.

Gus said to me, "They say you're fighting Augie Sanchez."

Las Vegas was too big a city for rumor to travel like gossip. My dad shook my hand, said, "Tommy," and I said, "Gus." He was dressed in one of those black suits from the fifties. You know, narrow shiny pants, the jacket short on the hip and in the sleeves. He had on a white-on-white shirt and skinny black tie. He'd either driven a funeral this morning or planned to do one later. He retired officially ten years ago. The man owned ten mortuaries in Las Vegas, but he still drove some funerals for the hell of it. Gus put on a cap and the suit and stood around like a chauffeur. He got a kick out of being the help, and no one ever recognized him for the boss he was. His way of meeting you was he'd say, I may not look like a million bucks, but don't judge a book by its jacket.

"So," Gus said, "you and Augie. Two Las Vegas boys hammering it out."

I said, "That's a story someone's telling."

"It isn't true?" he said.

"It isn't true in any way," I said.

He had a lunch for us on the patio that overlooked his backyard. He'd made tuna sandwiches, laid out potato chips and sliced cheese, three kinds, cheddar, Swiss, colby. He'd cut the blocks in squares the size of dice. I think you could have bought a car for what Gus's patio furniture cost. We could see most of Las Vegas from where we sat. The city was swelling, four thousand people a month moving in. Dad's lawn dropped three tiers to his swimming pool, and a lap pool ran along the fence. He landscaped the yard himself, no grass. It was all desert and cactus and olive trees.

"Your mother didn't want to see you fight," he said. Sitting there, he pretended to slip a punch. "We'd hear you won, though, and I'd see her smile. She asked after the details, and I told her what I heard." He crossed his legs like he was going to talk about his shoes. "Third round, I'd say. Upper cut, upper cut, overhand right. The boys'd tell me. Plugg'd call."

I helped Gus clear our plates, and he started setting up for chess. It was what we did Sundays. He kept his game nearby in a cabinet. He said, "She'd say, 'Gus, you go ahead. I know you'd like to see your boy.' I'd shake her off, and we'd wait to hear what happened. I couldn't sit still in the house. I'd go from room to room or I'd wander the neighborhood. Later she'd find my cigars, lit and unsmoked, in five or six ashtrays. We were two wrecks waiting on the news."

I sat on my side of the board, and it hit me that Gus's cocker Vic hadn't greeted me. Vic—Vic for Victory—and I, we had a friend-ship. I was his roughhousing buddy. I said, "Where's Vic?"

Dad moved a pawn, and I countered with my own. He'd whip me. Who'd win wasn't a question.

"I went to the vet yesterday," Dad said. "I had to pick up heart pills. It's on the calendar. Heart pills written out and a small red heart. Your mother did that every year. January one, she'd put up new calendars. First she'd go through and write down birthdays, all the days she needed to remember. So, is your father dumb? No, I'm a student. I learn. I keep my own log." He shrugged and moved another pawn. "I'm at the vet, and I'm waiting to pay, test-ing the collars they've got on a rack—solid clasp? long enough? You remember your mother on collars. I see the toothpaste. Edna did that, too. She brushed Vic's teeth. Makes me feel guilty. I keep thinking I should do it."

I felt guilty, and I wasn't even around.

He said, "There's this electronic sign in there that flashes messages and pictures. It's on the wall behind the counter. It showed a dog scooting on its butt and said, 'Is your dog scooting?' The dog scoots across the sign, like that singer. You've seen him, that kid who used to sing with his family. Now he's had all those surgeries on his face and is worth about fifty million. You know that step he does?"

I said I did.

Dad said, "He goes backward though. The dog scoots forward."

"Is that bad?" I braved my queen.

He said, "I told the girl when I paid for the pills. I said Vic is doing that, and I pointed at the sign. She called Park out. I told Park what Vic's doing, sort of showed him, and Park tells me to bring him in. It could be he just needs me to squeeze him. Park tells me he can show me how to do it, only I didn't want to know. So I had Ginger take Vic over, and she left him. Park wasn't there."

I said, "Squeeze what?"

"You don't want to know," Gus said. "Your mother used to say, I should know from trouble as much as I know about that." He indicated it was my move.

I put my queen in retreat. I'd risked her, let her out early, and it was too late.

Gus said, "Now it's Sunday, and they're closed."

Two moves later he checkmated me.

At the front door, I told Gus I'd pick up Vic first thing Monday morning and take him on a job with me. Gus said, "I think your mother wanted to see you fight. There was a big part of her thought she shouldn't want to. It wasn't womanly, and she was a lady. She always said she couldn't stand to see you get hurt."

"Hearing about it was probably enough," I said.

"I'd give her the blow-by-blow. Second-hand," he said. "Truth is, I think she didn't want to see you hurting someone else."

"She had that kind of heart," I said.

"I stayed away for her, I guess," he said.

We walked out to my car, not talking. I opened the door and said, "That was as good a reason as any."

"But I'm not sure that's true," he said. He rubbed his face like he was trying to erase it. He messed up his hair. He said, "So you're not fighting Sanchez?"

"I'm not," I said. "Not in a million years."

He said, "Plugg thought you were."

"Plugg imagines a lot of things."

You can shingle a roof at night if you have to. All you need is enough light to keep from tripping. Get your bearings, and a course laid in, and it's a matter of lay and staple.

I tell you this not because I was doing a night job but so you know how mindless the roof was I did Monday morning. It was asphalt shingles, a new church out on Decatur, low and long stretches, no pitch to speak of. I'd already done most of it and had come to finish up. My partner didn't show. Too many bars between his place and the job, and I didn't want to hunt him down. You see me up there, and you're right to think you know me. You can't imagine I've read anything that counts, that I could tell you how and why the planets align themselves. You can't imagine me and you talking about the important subjects you know.

Lunch came, and I sat on a pallet of cement bags next to a set-back spot of grass where I'd tied Vic to a pipe. The dog had it made in the shade. I hosed him down every hour, and for a while a row of sprinklers came on and sent a mist his way. All I had left was flashing to fit to a mid-roof chimney. I stripped my knee pads clean off and said to Vic, "Maybe another hour." I tossed him bits of cheese from the sandwich I'd brought. I freshened the water in his bowl.

A tall lean kid—maybe twenty, but only by a day or two—ambled over and said, "They tell me you're Tommy Rooke." I'd seen him earlier laying tile in the foyer.

I said, "They?"

"The guys I work with." He turned toward the van he'd arrived in. Three goofballs were looking our way.

I said, "They told you right."

He wore dusty harness boots and a cap.

You've seen this scene. It's been written. It's been painted. It's been filmed. Young greenhorn, wet-behind-the-ears kid gets goaded into saying, *They tell me you're Billy the Kid.* Billy, holding three jacks, doesn't respond. Greenhorn says, *They say you're fast with a gun. They say you killed over a hundred men.* Billy, he's bored and impatient and unflappable, and besides he's holding a winning hand, kings and an ace high, and there's fifty bucks in the pot, so, gun out of his holster, spun and its handle cracking the kid across the temple, he bushwhacks the hick before the greenhorn gets one more word out. Or, today's version, you know, is Yuppies in a bar. One of them was a boxer at Princeton. You know the rest. Ends with blood on his Oxford button-down.

This greenhorn says to me, "They said you're making a comeback."

"I don't know who they are," I said. "On the other hand, they got it wrong." I tossed cheese to Vic. I asked the kid his name, and he said it was Joseph, after his father. He said, "No one calls me Joe."

I said, "Why don't you sit down? Plenty of room," and I indicated the cement bags.

He glanced over at the crew. They'd gathered by their van, seemed to be calling it a day. Two were loading in their wet saw.

"Unless you're leaving," I said.

He said he couldn't. Not yet. He didn't sit. He said, "I fight."

"In the ring?" I said.

"Not so far," he said. "I'm in training."

He hadn't fought, not for real. If he had, he'd be lifting one leg out of deference here and using the other one to hop in the direction he came from. Joseph had never eaten a punch. He looked at his crew again. What he needed was a cold shower.

He said, "I was wondering if you had any pointers."

"Not in this heat," I said.

He chewed his lip.

I said, "You have questions?"

He didn't understand me.

"From your boys?" I said.

He still didn't get it.

I said, "Do you know anything about computers?"

He stared at me like I'd brought up a joke and he was saying, *So, how's it go?*

I got to my feet, and I said, "My brain isn't wired for chess." I collected Vic's water bowl and tossed the water on the dirt. I said, "My dad beats me every Sunday. I go over there and we talk, and then he embarrasses me at chess." I was running fresh water in Vic's bowl, so I talked a little louder. I said, "He's been following the game between that genius and the computer. You know who I mean?"

The kid shook his head, saying *no* and also saying, *Where are you going with this?*

I said, "It's a name sounds like a guy who'd play chess. One of those Russian-sounding names. He's American, I think."

"I don't know," the kid said.

"Big Blue is what they call the computer," I said.

The kid shuffled in the dirt. His crew had finished loading and were loafing by their van. They kept glancing our way.

"What I'm getting to," I said, "is that my dad tells me the computer won't ever win because it can't learn from its mistakes. It might win a game or two. No way, though, Big Blue will ever win a match. I'm quoting my dad here."

The kid said, "I don't know anything about chess."

I shut the water off and twirled what hose I'd used back into its circle. I gave Vic a hug, and from where I'd crouched I said, "I thought someone might have told you boxing is like chess." I stood and said, "It isn't. Not in any way you can think."

His crew honked, and the kid said, "I got to go. Best of luck, if you fight."

I didn't have anything else to say, so he turned and walked away.

Around seven I drove Vic home, and Ginger talked me into taking her to the Southtown Mall. She wanted what she called big-ass shoes. Her ear looked like shit. She told me Snyder took her to Doc's and she refused to go in. I wrote a note for Gus. The vet diagnosed Vic as having paper foot. My note said, "That's why he walks like he has pins in his feet." I wrote, "He should stop scooting. Keep an eye on him." I didn't say anything about Gus learning to squeeze Vic's butt. One day I'd show Gus how, before he could object. Before he could throw up his hands. I'd lay guilt on thick, say, *Do you suppose Edna would hesitate? Would Edna let a potential problem get worse out of negligence?* Gus'd give in.

Ginger and I stopped at Cal's on the Boulder Highway. Cal's looks like a cracker box outside. Inside it opens up. There's snooker in a back room. There's a bar. There's a lunch counter. The parlor itself is divided so one side is for locals, and there's space for people who can play the game. There's even a pro shop.

Everywhere I'd gone today there'd been a message from Plugg. Can we meet? Got to see you. He'd be at Cal's.

Sure enough, we found him in the back, deep into a game of one pocket. We took seats with the other rail birds. You could smell the money riding on this game. Plugg's stroke was off. May have been legitimate or he might have been hustling this sporty-looking dude I'd never seen before. Plugg was acting like Lady Luck was using his stick when he made a shot. The other guy was tall, heavy. He'd have to size up a doorway before stepping through it. Had his hair in a ponytail. You could see Plugg lagging and then locking up the cue ball. He dinked around, then suddenly said, "Duck soup," and ran seven to the finish. Next next next. The guy shook Plugg's hand and said, "That's one damn tight table."

"Go again?" Plugg said.

The guy said, "I'm out of sync. Another day."

Plugg turned to me and Ginger, pocketing his money, and said, "I got drinks." He said, "Hey, Ginger."

She said, "Paisley."

Plugg shook his head, baffled.

"I'm Paisley," Ginger said. "Call me Paisley."

I helped Plugg into his suit coat, and we went out front where there was a bar and booths. He guided us to a booth, then went for drinks. He didn't ask what we wanted.

"You going to fight?" Ginger said.

I told her I couldn't think of one reason to.

She told me it was the only thing Gus talked about. "We go out to dinner last night," she said, "and he's all, 'Your brother, he could dance. Move over Muhammad Ali.' He's all, 'Your brother packed a wallop.'"

She knew he never saw me fight. She was talking like she

wasn't around in those days. Nine, ten, eleven—that was old enough to know your brother was a fighter. She touched her ear—it looked swollen, was red as an apple—and said, "Is he making things up?"

"I never lost," I said.

She said, "That's no answer."

I said, "Not a mark on me," and I gave her a slow wink.

"You're not talking, is that it?" she said.

Plugg arrived with our drinks. "Coke, Paisley?" he said to Ginger and set one down in front of her.

"Perfect," she said.

He handed me a Club Soda, saying, "All I need is your okay. I can lock this up today."

I sipped my drink.

"What are the magic words?" he said. "Abracadabra? Do-wah, Do-wah, Do-wah Ditty?" He sat across from me and Ginger. He drank rum and Coke. He said, "I'm up front with you since the day I walked into your life. You'll admit to this, no? Not one incident or occurrence of me speaking out of the side of my mouth, of Plugg looking one way and going in another direction altogether." He noticed Ginger tug her ear. "Dear," he said, "you'll make it worse."

She went back to her Coke.

A thug named Hammond, passing, said to Plugg, "I'm waiting on you making good."

Plugg said to him, "You're not standing and you're not flying."

"If push comes to shove," Hammond said.

Plugg said, "Shtarker." *Tough guy.*

"Sure," Hammond said. He went into the men's room.

"So," Plugg said to me, "day one, you and me, what you see is what you get. Now, see, things are different. Not between you and me." He put his hands together to show how buddy-buddy we were. "Hey, they cut you, I bleed. In the fight game, is what I mean. All is change, all is change. It's hardly worth the trouble anymore. Now it's who you hold hands with. Not that x can do y for z wasn't always the means to the end. Now, though, see, x wants to get to z, only y's in the way."

I said, "How am I y?"

"Tommy, Tommy," Plugg said, "no one's saying you're y."

Behind us there was the click of pool balls.

Plugg sipped his rum and Coke. He leaned into the table. "Forget your x and your y and your z. We want back in the fight game, and the whole story is another way around, you understand. I tell the guys I'm negotiating. You don't know how bleeped up it all is." He smiled at Ginger, said, "Don't touch." He half-swatted her hand from her ear.

I said, "Plugg, who are you negotiating with?"

"Tommy," he said, "have I ever taken you down the garden path? Told you one thing and meant another?"

Plugg was fitting his A's to his B's to his C's.

I let him set the table. The upshot was I fight Sanchez and win or lose I take to the bank a shitload of money. Sanchez earns— Plugg's word—five times what I do. "You understand how it works," Plugg said. "Your name, five months, these people don't know who you are, were. You've been out now six, seven years. Down the line, things, they're different."

Plugg finished, and Ginger said to me, "Why not?"

I said, "It's a long story."

Ginger said, "Not if you don't tell it." She touched her ear and said, "It's a simple yes or no."

Plugg said, "What our planet needs more of, a young lady who tells it like it is."

I told Plugg to give me two days to think. We had to sign by Friday, and the fight would be nine months away.

Here's the question for you, and it's not a trick one. It's multiple choice. Circle the correct answer.

It's the third round, and the fight's scheduled for twelve. You've cut your opponent's eye and it's closing up. You shredded it. His blood coats your gloves. It mats the hair on your arms. There is blood splattered on the rich folks, the celebrities in the front-row seats, the tuxedoed men and the women in gowns. This guy can't see, and he keeps coming at you. He's swinging blind.

What do you do?

Circle the correct answer.

(a) Pick at the eye. Jab. Jab. Jab.
(b) Tie him up and turn him so the referee can't ignore the damage you've done. Embarrass the referee into stopping the fight.
(c) Chew your gloves off and walk out of the ring.
(d) Take a dive.

There's only one correct answer.

Go ahead.

ACKNOWLEDGMENTS

I'd like to express thanks to Kate, who reads with a scalpel; to François Camoin and Rob Roberge, whose rigor is contagious; to Bruce Jorgensen, for walking and talking; and to Eddie and Hirsch.

I'd like to thank the following journals for publishing some of the stories in this collection: "Blood Work," *The Antioch Review*; "The 12-Inch Dog," *Epoch*; "Caution: Men in Trees," *The Gettysburg Review*; "Please to Forgive Sloppiness" and "Late-Night TV," *High Plains Literary Review*; "It's a Lot Scarier If You Take Jesus Out," *Shenandoah*; "Pronto Bucks," *Indiana Review*; "There's Too Much News," *Web Del Sol*.

THE FLANNERY O'CONNOR AWARD
FOR SHORT FICTION